MAYWOOD PUBLIC LIBRARY
W9-CER-026

Discovering Martha

Joanne Rocklin

Discovering Martha

MACMILLAN PUBLISHING COMPANY
New York

Maxwell Macmillan Canada
Toronto

Maxwell Macmillan International
New York Oxford Singapore Sydney

Acknowledgment
The author is most grateful to Dr. Thomas Santulli, Director of Pediatrics at Cedars-Sinai Medical Center, Los Angeles, for his generous assistance.

Macmillan Publishing Company is part of the Maxwell Communication Group of Companies.

Macmillan Publishing Company
866 Third Avenue, New York, NY 10022

Maxwell Macmillan Canada, Inc.
1200 Eglinton Avenue East, Suite 200, Don Mills, Ontario M3C 3N1

First edition
Printed in the United States of America
10 9 8 7 6 5 4 3 2 1
The text of this book is set in 12.5 point Berkeley Old Style.

Library of Congress Cataloging-in-Publication Data
Rocklin, Joanne.
Discovering Martha / Joanne Rocklin. — 1st ed.
p. cm.
Summary: Does the mysterious purple guitar possess magic or does learning to play it merely motivate Martha, a sixth-grader going through an awkward stage, to change her life a little?
ISBN 0-02-777444-9
[1.Guitar—Fiction.] I.Title.
PZ7.R59Di 1991 [Fic.]—dc20 91-18973

For my sisters, Karen Gaiger and Ellen Rocklin

One

WHEN she was four and a half years old, Martha Green was discovered in the meat department of the L.A. Food Mart. Choosing groceries with her mom had given Martha a happy, warm, sing-a-song kind of feeling. And so Martha began to sing "Old Macdonald Had a Farm," one of her favorites. She started singing about the chickens, then went on to the cows and the lambs, loudly and clearly, putting her finger cutely to her cheek when other shoppers smiled and said, "How sweet!"

But then, as she helped her mother push their cart toward the meat department with its rows and rows of plastic-wrapped packages of chicken legs and rump roasts and lamb chops, a thought occurred to Martha right in the middle of her ee-eye-ee-eye-ohing: Those packages used to be farm animals! Live ones.

Martha began to cry. Her mother explained that human beings, meat eaters for the most part, had to get their food somewhere. But Martha continued crying, thinking about the poor animals clucking and mooing and baaing their songs, just as she herself had been doing. She would have cried longer, but all of a sudden a woman wearing a big hat with oranges and grapes and strawberries on it pushed her cart beside theirs. The wonderful hat fascinated Martha and she stopped crying. She wondered why the woman was putting her fruit on top of her hat instead of into her basket.

Then the woman leaned over to Mrs. Green and said, "Madam, you have an adorable child, blessed with an appreciation for the drama of life."

The oranges and grapes and strawberries on the woman's hat turned out to be plastic. The woman herself turned out to be Mrs. Fifer, a Hollywood talent scout, and their meeting led to Martha's small parts in commercials as a Souper Soup eater when she was five and a Wendy Wet owner when she was six.

But when Martha was seven, things started changing. Mr. Green had some business and money problems, and the Greens had to count every penny and sell their house and move into the Mariella Manor apartment complex. Martha's oldest sister, Sabrina, started college, and Mrs. Green went to work as an executive secretary to help pay for things. She had much less time to take Martha to auditions for commercials, which weren't coming up as often, anyway. Mrs. Fifer called less and less as Martha grew bigger, and, Martha assumed, less adorable. Then, when Martha turned eleven, Martha's other sister, Kimberly, started college, and Mr. and Mrs. Green had to work harder than ever.

Martha longed to be discovered again. And if a person could be discovered twice in her life, Martha decided that the next time she would change her name to Mariella Emerald instead of remaining just plain Martha Green. Mariella was the name of the daughter of the man who owned the Mariella Manor apartments. (Her parents had been told that when they signed the lease.) Martha thought that Mariella Emerald was the most beautiful name in the whole world. A person would become beautiful just having that name. Perhaps things would have been different if it had been her name from the very beginning.

Already she had asked her parents to change the family name to Emerald, but they had absolutely refused.

"Grandpa Green changed *his* name from Greenburger," she said. "I don't see why you can't make one more change to Emerald."

"One change is enough," her father had said.

As Mariella Emerald, star, thought Martha, walking slowly home from Cypress Tree Avenue Elementary School one afternoon, she would make piles of money so her parents could retire, or at least come home earlier, and maybe buy a big house on the other side of the boulevard, where many of the students from her school lived. As Mariella Emerald, star, she would have lots and lots of friends, as stars always do.

Ahead of her walked Jennifer Okuda, the new girl. Martha remembered that Jennifer hadn't received one of Tiffany Oliver's Halloween pumpkin bash invitations, which Tiffany had handed out at recess time to the most popular sixth graders. Martha felt very sorry for Jennifer Okuda and hurried to catch up. She herself hadn't received an invitation, either, but she hadn't expected one, just as she hadn't expected one the previous year, or the year before that. It must be harder to be left out if you were new, she thought.

Martha caught up with Jennifer and began a conversation. Suddenly, she decided to tell a lie. Maybe it was because deep in her heart she *had* been hoping to be invited to Tiffany's annual pumpkin bash, and felt a bit sad. Or maybe it was because Jennifer seemed like a very nice person to have as a best friend, or because Martha's parents would be working late and Martha wished she weren't going home alone. It wasn't an outright black lie and it wasn't a little white lie (generally used when she didn't want to hurt anyone's feelings). It was in-between (charcoal gray), and it ruined everything.

"Sometimes it's so hard being a star," remarked Martha casually during a lull in the conversation, as she and Jennifer walked home together.

Jennifer glanced at Martha with interest.

"You really lose your privacy." Martha sighed. "You can't even go into a store without someone coming up to you for your autograph or interviewing you about your life and what you had for breakfast."

Martha closed her eyes, as if to block out a bad memory. "Or you could be at the movies or the supermarket or something, or maybe just playing in the park, enjoying the nice weather like any other citizen of the United States, and someone will yell out something to you, really loudly. It gets annoying after a while."

"You sound like you've been through all that yourself," said Jennifer.

Martha looked down at her feet modestly, even though she had been hoping very much that Jennifer would say something like that. Then Martha put her finger to her cheek and cocked her head to the side. " 'Wendy cries, Wendy sleeps, Wendy even wets!' " She paused and looked expectantly at Jennifer. "Ring a bell?"

Jennifer was quiet for a moment. "I don't think so," she said finally.

"How about 'Hey, Mom, this soup's soo-per!' " Martha sang, and then slurped noisily from an imaginary spoon.

"Not really," said Jennifer.

"They're TV commercials!" cried Martha. "When I

was in kindergarten I did a Souper Soup commercial, and when I was in first grade I did a Wendy Wet commercial."

Jennifer shook her head. "I really don't remember you," she said in a kind voice.

"That's okay," said Martha sadly. "Hardly anybody else remembers me, either."

Then Martha felt ashamed of bragging to Jennifer Okuda and hinting, with her charcoal-gray lie, that she used to be a star.

"I've kind of changed in five years," she said. "I used to be adorable." Martha looked down at her size 7½ sneakers. "I've grown. A lot. And I'm a few pounds overweight, as you can see." With an embarrassed smile, she pointed to a popped-open button dangling by a thread from the waist of her skirt.

Jennifer didn't seem to notice the loose button. "It must have been so much fun to be in commercials!" she exclaimed.

"Oh, it was!" said Martha, remembering the cameras and the bright lights and all the good food on the set. "It definitely was."

Tiffany Oliver was waiting at the boulevard for the light to change.

"Martha was just telling me how she used to be a star," said Jennifer. "How people used to ask for her autograph and interview her and call out to her in parks."

"Martha, that's a big, fat lie, and you know it!" cried Tiffany.

"I didn't exactly say all that happened to me *personally*," mumbled Martha, feeling her ears turning red.

Jennifer gave a little gasp of disapproval.

"But I really *was* in two commercials!" said Martha quickly.

"It wasn't as if you were making movies or were a regular on your own TV show or something." Tiffany leaned toward Jennifer as if Martha weren't even there. "Martha is a show-off and an exaggerator. Every single person in the class says so, even the teacher."

"That's not true! Miss Marshall *never* said I was a show-off."

"Okay, *I* say you're a show-off. Miss Marshall says you're an exaggerator." Tiffany pressed the button hard for the crosswalk light, two times, as if she couldn't stand to be talking to such a person one more second of her life.

"But once a lady *did* come up to me in the supermarket when I happened to be standing next to the soup section. And she *did* ask me some very personal questions."

Actually, Martha remembered with a twinge of guilt, the lady merely asked Martha her age and soup preference, since her grandchildren were about Martha's age and were coming for a visit. But Martha liked to think it was also because the lady recognized her from TV.

"If things had been a little different," said Martha, her hands on her hips defiantly, "maybe I *could* have been a star! A big one!"

Tiffany and Jennifer giggled. "A big one!" mimicked Tiffany, her hands on her hips, too.

The light turned green. "Bye," said Jennifer coolly, stepping off the curb to cross the boulevard with Tiffany.

Martha stood at the corner for several minutes, blinking back tears. "I am blessed with an appreciation for the drama of life!" she suddenly shouted to no one in particular, for by that time Tiffany and Jennifer were two small specks in the distance.

Martha gave a big sigh and continued on her way home. Jennifer would never want to be best friends now, she thought to herself. Oh, so what? Having a best friend, as far as she could see, made your life very complicated. You had to tell a best friend everything, every single private thing in your life, down to the nitty-gritty details like what you had for breakfast. You had to do your homework together. And you had to talk on the phone a lot, which took up so much time. It just wasn't worth it.

Martha turned down her street, Forest Glen Drive, lost in thought. And what if, just say, Martha became one of the popular girls? That, too, would make her life very complicated. Because if she were one of the popular girls, she'd have to wear pretty, boutique-bought clothes every single day, in the exact same color that the rest of the group was wearing. That was what Tiffany and her friends liked to do, and it was certainly out of the question for Martha, who was stuck wearing her older sisters' hand-me-downs much of the time. Her parents were so careful and practical, what with all their business and money problems, and college, and saving for their retirement.

When she reached Mariella Manor at the end of the block, Martha slipped the key chain from around her neck and unlocked the door to the lobby. She picked up her family's mail, then regarded the rusty suggestion box attached to the mailboxes. She wondered, as she always did, who read the suggestions, and if anyone else besides Martha made any. None of *her* suggestions were ever carried out. But you never know, thought Martha hopefully. She tore a piece of paper from one of her school notebooks.

"I suggest," she wrote, using the pencil stub attached by an old piece of string to a nail, "that beautiful music be piped into the lobby, following us into the elevator. I suggest that we hang a big bulletin board near the mailboxes for inter-tenant communication. I also suggest that all Mariella Manor tenants chip in to purchase lottery tickets. Winnings to be split equally among us, of course." She signed it, "A Tenant, Martha Green."

If she was discovered again, she might be able to earn quite a bit of money, Martha thought. Maybe even more than she would get from the lottery. Then her parents wouldn't have to work so hard. Their worries would be over. They could all fly off to Tahiti, as her father often said he longed to do. Wearing bright, flowered clothes, they would eat strange fruit and dance on the beach under a round, yellow moon, just like the travelers in the airline commercials.

Martha stepped into the elevator and pressed 3, turning to scrutinize herself in the elevator's mirror. Nothing adorable about her now, that was for sure. Even her name was unadorable. Martha. *Mar-tha.* A two-syllable name, like two heavy footsteps, plod, plod. Three- and four-syllable names skipped merrily along, wearing pretty dancing slippers. *Jeh-ni-fur. Tih-fuh-nee. Mar-ee-eh-la.*

Martha threw back her head, tossed her hair, and laughed into the elevator mirror, just as she had once seen an actress do on TV. Then she turned to one side and winked at herself. She put a finger to her cheek. She clapped her hands and did a couple of zippy dance steps from one end of the elevator to the other, in perfect rhythm to imaginary piped-in music.

The doors opened at the third floor.

"Excuse *me!*" said a voice, as Martha was skipping out of the elevator backward, blowing kisses to an imaginary audience.

Martha turned and smiled sheepishly at the tenant from 308. "Sorry," she murmured, feeling her face getting red. "Just pretending something."

The tenant from 308 was a stylishly dressed man always in a hurry, whose name Martha couldn't remember. He entered the elevator and bent down to wipe his stepped-upon shoe. "I recommend less pretending and more attention to what's going on around you," he said as the doors closed.

Martha stuck out her tongue at the closed elevator doors. "What a crab," she said out loud.

So what if she pretended—pretended that she had a best friend to talk over nitty-gritties with; that she was still adorable; that her parents were rich, and they lived in a big one-family house across the boulevard instead of in Mariella Manor, where hardly anyone knew anyone else, or wanted to. And pretended, no, *wished* with all her heart, that she was Mariella Emerald, discovered again, instead of just plain Martha Green.

Two

THAT'S strange, thought Martha. Leaning near the door to the Greens' apartment was a very large carton. "To Resident" was written on the box in purple ink, followed by the Greens' address on Forest Glen Drive. The box seemed like a great big piece of junk mail, the kind that her parents, looking annoyed, threw away without opening.

Martha unlocked the door, plunked her books onto the kitchen table, and then went back to get the box. She couldn't imagine what was inside. It looked official and important, festooned with colorful stamps. At the top left-hand corner of the box was the return address: 1234 Tuneful Trail, Suite 10, Via del Mar, California.

Martha didn't know anybody from a place called Via del Mar. The package was most certainly for her mother and father. Of course she couldn't open it. The Greens never, ever opened one another's mail, respecting each one's privacy to the utmost. Not that

Martha got much mail, except for occasional letters from her sisters or a birthday card, usually in the wrong month, from her grandfather Green, who had a memory problem. But someday, Martha hoped, she would receive very private mail, such as love letters. At times like that, she would appreciate more than ever how her family never, ever opened one another's mail.

She carried the box into the living room and leaned it against the couch. Near the telephone was the usual note from her mother: MARTHA, CASSEROLE IN OVEN AT 6 O'CLOCK, 350 DEGREES.

Martha sighed as she read the label on the casserole. Mushroom pot roast. Bor-ing.

She understood why her busy and efficient mother cooked and froze the same seven casseroles ahead of time. But it would be so much fun, thought Martha, her head in the pantry as she searched for a snack, to have a mom like that gourmet cook on TV, a daring woman in a sari who flipped omelets and presented new, exotic dishes every single week.

Martha spotted the bag of Halloween candy. She had asked her mother to buy it, even though her mother had reminded her that nobody but Winston Hooper from upstairs ever came trick-or-treating at Mariella Manor, and that Martha would end up eating it herself.

"I won't touch it!" Martha had declared, having

begun a new diet that very afternoon. But what was Halloween without candy? It was like Thanksgiving without turkey. You had to have candy around the house at Halloween. "It's an important tradition," she had said. And what if crowds of children rang their doorbell that year, and they had nothing at all to give them? That would be awful, absolutely awful!

Martha peeled off a black Halloween wrapper and popped a piece of orange goo into her mouth. When she finished that piece, she ate two more. She could smell the smell of that morning's breakfast, a lonely smell when it reminded you that you were the first one home. She listened to the refrigerator's hum, a lonely sound when there were no other noises. Martha reached for another piece of candy and jumped when the telephone rang.

"Hi, it's me," said Winston Hooper. "I'm coming down."

"You could at least ask," said Martha.

"Why? What're you doing?"

"Nothing much. Eating. But why do you always *assume* that I'm not busy? In fact, I've got piles and piles of homework to do which I'm going to begin immediately. Sorry, Win."

After she had hung up, Martha could hear Winston's footsteps thumping overhead. Probably on purpose, so she'd feel sorry for him. It was such a burden being someone's best friend when you didn't feel the same way back. The only reason Winston wanted to be her friend was that he didn't live near anyone from his school, the Hollyhock Academy for the Highly Gifted. What if she had her own best friend over, say, Jennifer Okuda? What if they were trying to do their homework together and they couldn't concentrate because of the racket Winston Hooper was making upstairs? It would be so embarrassing!

"That Winston! He drives me crazy!" confided Martha out loud to a pretend Jennifer.

Winston thumped again and Martha began to feel bad. Winston said he didn't care that he didn't have any friends from school who lived near him, but Martha didn't really believe him. Winston said he liked attending the Hollyhock Academy for the Highly Gifted because he got to wear a uniform that made him feel strong and brave, like a soldier. And he said he didn't care that he lived alone with his divorced mother, who treated him like a baby, because she bought him anything he wanted.

"I'm overprotected," he told Martha. "But you know why."

Martha tried not to think about why, but she couldn't help remembering poor Winston's too-narrow heart valves and his operation, which was coming up. Winston had told her there was always a chance that he wouldn't pull through. Even though

Martha's parents had said that the situation was more hopeful than that, and even though Winston was annoying a lot of the time, she felt she should try to be kinder to him. Besides, he was the only kid she knew so far who remembered her Souper Soup commercial.

Martha dialed Winston's number. "Oh, all right, come down," she said, and not more than one minute later, her doorbell was ringing furiously.

Winston wasn't wearing his school uniform. Instead, he was dressed all in black, from big black boots and black cape to a strange, black, spiked headdress fitted with a bicycle light that flashed and emitted chirping beeps every few seconds. Triangles of red construction paper were stapled to his shoulders. He stood at the door, arms stiffly at his sides, muffled music playing, it seemed to Martha, from his armpits.

"But Halloween is next week," she said, holding back a giggle.

"I know," said Winston, "but I wanted to perfect my costume before the big night. Do you think I'm authentic looking?"

Before Martha could answer, he lifted up his black shirt and scratched under a belt strapped around his skinny chest. The belt held two twin transistor radios at each end.

"Boy, this itches! First it tickles, then it itches."

Winston tightened the musical belt and pulled his shirt down again as he came beeping into the apartment. "You know who I am, don't you?"

"Give me a hint."

" 'Dark as eternity and fearless as the night is long.' "

"Hmm. . . ."

" 'He walks with fire. The music of the gods surrounds him.' "

"No-o-o. . . ."

Winston frowned. "Gee, I thought it was so obvious. I'm Volpa! From *The Scourge of the Universe.*"

"You know I don't read that science fiction stuff!" exclaimed Martha. Then she burst out laughing as Winston's radios switched from music to fried-chicken commercials.

Winston sighed and turned off the radios. "The music part has some flaws. I really wanted to buy two small tape recorders, but my mom said that was going a bit too far. I guess it's a stupid costume," he said, sitting down on the couch.

"It's a great costume, Win," said Martha, sorry that she'd laughed at him. She reached over to touch one of Winston's red paper triangles. "I like the flames."

"Thanks," said Winston, brightening.

"Here, have some Halloween candy." Martha sat down on the couch beside him, taking two more pieces herself. "We really bought this stuff for you, since you're the only person who'll be trick-or-treating around these parts."

"But you said you were coming with me!" cried Winston. "That's the only way my mother will let me leave Mariella Manor without her!"

"There's a Halloween party that night, a pumpkin bash," said Martha guiltily. Her second charcoal-gray lie of the day. But still, a lot could happen between then and Halloween. You never could tell.

"Aw, Marth," said Winston. He looked at her reproachfully.

Martha had to admit that trick-or-treating with your mom when you were in sixth grade wasn't something to look forward to. And what if it *was* Winston's last Halloween? Chances were that it wouldn't be, but *what if it was?* She would never, ever forgive herself.

"Oh, okay. Before the party. For a little while."

"Great!" Winston took a piece of candy. He noticed the big box by the couch. "What's that?"

"Something for my parents," mumbled Martha with her mouth full.

Just then the phone rang. It was Mrs. Hooper, asking to speak to her son.

Winston frowned into the receiver. "Mom, I already finished my homework. Yes, I practiced, but I put my clarinet away and that's why it looks like I didn't. No, *more* than five minutes. Aw, Mom!"

Poor Winston, thought Martha. He had to practice

twice a day. His mom was so strict, even though she bought him anything he wanted.

"I have to go home to finish practicing," said Winston. He shook his fist at the ceiling. "I hate my clarinet with a passion!"

Winston's beeps faded into the distance as he took the elevator upstairs. Soon Martha heard clarinet toots instead. She wondered what it felt like to have a mother who watched you every minute, instead of parents who respected your privacy to the utmost.

After Winston's noisy visit, the apartment seemed quieter and lonelier than ever. Martha's parents wouldn't be home for another two hours. She turned on the television set. A man was discussing a movie that he did not like at all. She changed the channel and watched a cartoon, eating three more pieces of candy. How did half the bag get eaten so quickly? She should start her homework, she realized. She really *did* have piles and piles to do.

Martha pulled her math book from her knapsack and began to work on some problems. During a particularly tricky calculation, as she was chewing on her pencil and staring into space, she noticed the big box again. What could be in it? What if she opened it up and took a very quick look inside? The box said "To Resident." Well, wasn't she a resident, too?

Martha carried the box into her bedroom and

snipped off its heavy string with a pair of scissors. She tore away the sticky tape wrapped around the edges of the box. Then she dug deep down through layers of paper.

What she found at the bottom made her gasp with surprise and joy.

Three

IT was a guitar, plum purple and shiny.

Martha lifted it carefully from the guitar case. She breathed in its smell of newness, unlike any smell she had ever smelled before. She stroked the guitar's glossy surface, then traced the black curlicues looping up the sides. The guitar was so shiny, she could see her blurry but excited face peering back at her.

Who was it for? Martha tried to imagine her parents, who were older than the other moms and dads she knew, playing this flashy, purple guitar. Bernard Green, preoccupied and serious, his briefcase stuffed with work and money problems. Busy, tired Vivien Green in her sensible shoes, so unlike the slim-heeled pumps or colorful sneakers that other mothers wore.

"No, no," whispered Martha, hugging the guitar close. "You were meant for me!"

Could it be a birthday present from Grandpa Green, sent by mistake? But her birthday was six whole months away.Oh, dear, thought Martha, who was very worried about her grandfather. Grandpa

Green *did* have trouble remembering important dates such as birthdays, as well as many other things. Sometimes he got lost in his own neighborhood near the beach and wandered up and down unfamiliar streets and alleys. Sometimes he didn't even remember to look at the address engraved on his silver bracelet, a present from the Greens.

But Grandpa Green said he hated today's music. He liked only yesterday's music, Yiddish folk tunes and pieces played by symphony orchestras. Just in case, Martha searched the box for a birthday card from her grandfather. There was none.

At the very bottom of the box, however, hidden beneath the layers of paper, was a little book. *The Guitar Player's Manual* was written in big purple letters on its cover. A folded note fell from its front pages, and Martha opened it.

"Dear Interested Party," she read. "Here is the instrument *you've been wishing you owned!* Six-week absolutely *Free* trial! Return if not satisfied! We guarantee you will learn to play in those *six short weeks!* Follow our *six easy exercises* using *The Marvelous Modern Method based on The Five Human Senses!* Experience the *magic* of playing a musical instrument! Be prepared to *delight and amaze* your family and friends! $200.00 Value for just $150.00! Only $99.99 Down! Easy Credit Terms! *Musical Enterprises.*"

It wasn't a gift from someone at all, thought Martha gloomily. One hundred and fifty dollars was less than two hundred dollars, but it was still a lot of money. Martha wasn't sure what easy credit meant, but she had a feeling that Interested Party still had to pay.

But six short weeks! And it was absolutely free during that time! That meant that she, Martha Green, would be a guitar player just in time for the holiday season.

Martha opened *The Guitar Player's Manual* and began to read:

> EXERCISE NUMBER ONE: *Introduction to the Guitar through the Sense of Touch.* Put the guitar strap over your head. Then hold your guitar as you would a bag of groceries in which the eggs were placed on top, i.e., proceed with confidence, but care. Do not hurry, for there is a wealth of possibilities in your grasp. *Savor the moment.* Study the drawing on this page.

Martha studied the computer-made drawing. Hundreds of tiny black dots, perfectly placed, created a smiling girl with flashing white teeth. Poised and confident, a girl who most likely possessed a three- or four-syllable name, she held a guitar just like Martha's.

Martha slipped the guitar strap over her head and held the guitar carefully in her arms. She looked at herself in her full-length mirror. "Be prepared," she whispered to the smiling and confident-looking girl she saw there. "Be prepared to delight and amaze!"

Oh, how wonderful that would be! She didn't delight or amaze anyone very often. It was understandable, of course. After all, she was her parents' *third* child. With Sabrina, their first, Vivien and Bernard Green had been delighted and amazed, for they had never been parents before. They took hundreds of photographs of Sabrina, right from the beginning up until the second she waved good-bye and left for college. And photographs of their second child, Kimberly, almost but not quite matched Sabrina's in number. But by the time their third child came along, Vivien and Bernard had seen it all, thought Martha. Except for a few baby pictures and the Souper Soup and Wendy Wet glossies, Martha's photo album had many blank pages and still crackled with newness when she opened it up.

Oh, yes, it was understandable. But sometimes, alone after school, Martha stared at her glossies for a long time, remembering the long-ago day when she had delighted the lady with the fruit-filled hat. She supposed she was a big disappointment, having lost all her adorableness.

Martha looked around her messy room. There were other reasons for her family to be disappointed in her. Scribbled-on papers and dusty cassette tapes, overdue library books and tangled marionettes were scattered about. Her bed was rumpled and unmade. She knew that several days' worth of socks and candy wrappers were tangled beneath it.

Martha was supposed to empty the Greens' waste-baskets every day, but she always waited until they were so full that she left a trail of apple cores and other trash all the way to the garbage chute. Further-more, she was often late for school, and her report cards were nothing to celebrate, certainly not as bril-liant as Sabrina's and Kimberly's used to be. Not that her busy parents complained much about any of this. They hardly even noticed.

"Please try to pick up," her mother usually said distractedly when she came into Martha's room.

"Keep up the good work," her father would say from behind his newspaper after glancing at her re-port card and its rows of plump C's.

But now she would be a guitar player! Martha began to dance around her bedroom, hugging the guitar and pretending to play it, twirling faster and faster until she was quite dizzy and the guitar was a bright, purple blur in the mirror. Finally Martha flopped down on her bed, the instrument beside her. She lay very still, listening to the pounding of her heart.

Experience the magic *of playing a musical instru-ment.*

The guitar had arrived out of nowhere. Poof! Just

like that. Now, wouldn't it be the most amazing thing, she thought, the most incredible and amazing thing, if this guitar were like the magic sticks and magic beans and magic pots that made wishes come true in storybooks?

Martha sat up. She closed her eyes and quickly rubbed the face of the guitar with her fingertips three times.

"Fee-fi-fo-fum! Alakazam-kazoo!" she shouted. "Make me . . . Mariella Emerald!"

Several long seconds went by. Martha flopped down on her bed again. Silly. If Tiffany and Jennifer had been watching, they would have had a nice, long laugh at her expense.

Martha sat up again. She touched the guitar's cool surface. But if the other exercises were as easy as Exercise Number One, she'd be a guitar player in no time. She would serenade her parents at the end of a hard day and they would all sing songs together. She would delight and amaze her friends and be invited to lots of parties. And maybe, just maybe, she would be discovered again!

Excited by the wealth of possibilities, Martha proceeded to the next exercise.

EXERCISE NUMBER TWO: *The Exquisite E Minor Chord and the Sense of Hearing.* (1) E minor is the easiest but most exquisite of chords. Press down the fingers of your left hand, as in the drawing on this page. (You may eventually develop calluses. These will be your "battle scars," Guitar Player.) At the same time, strum E minor with your right thumb, lovingly.

Martha examined the drawing of the confident-looking girl who was pressing with her left hand and strumming with her right thumb. She placed her fingers similarly on the neck of the guitar. Trying very hard not to be intimidated, she strummed as "lovingly" as she could.

(2) Now, listen to the exquisite sound you make! Keep listening with all your might as the music fills the air.

Well, the sound wasn't exquisite at all in Martha's opinion. She tried again and again, until finally she produced a small, sad sound. She played it many times, sometimes loudly, like a thunder clap, sometimes softly, like whispering rain. She kept listening and, sure enough, even when she stopped playing, the music seemed to hang in the air like mist. It was the loveliest sound Martha had ever heard, the sound of a feeling she had felt before but could never quite put into words.

(3) Chords have power, but beware—

Before Martha had a chance to read further, she heard a key in the lock. Quickly, almost without thinking, she put the purple guitar and the manual inside the guitar case, and the case inside the big box. Then she shoved the box under her bed and sat on top of the bed, just as her mother entered the apartment.

Four

OF course I'll show it to them, Martha told herself, sitting on top of her secret-under-the-bed. She wasn't entirely sure, however, whether it was a secret that *she* was keeping from her parents, or a wonderful secret her parents were keeping from *her*. Perhaps it *was* a present from her parents for obtaining C's regularly and doing her chores semiregularly.

But her parents didn't really believe in surprises, Martha remembered. Martha's parents always asked her what she wanted for birthdays and holidays weeks ahead of time, shopping from lists and looking for bargains. Once she had told her mother how Samantha Sampson's mom had bought Samantha a beautiful blouse with mirrored spangles on it as a surprise birthday present. Samantha had admired the blouse while shopping with Mrs. Sampson. Giggly Mrs. Sampson had bought it secretly that very day, hiding it away *for three whole months.*

"But what if Samantha had had a growth spurt and the blouse hadn't fit after three months! And mirrors!

Certainly not washable," practical Mrs. Green had commented, missing the entire point.

No, decided Martha. The purple guitar had arrived out of the blue, like a sample of soap powder or a magazine to try out until you decided whether you liked the product.

Frowning, Mrs. Green entered the bedroom. "You forgot to put the casserole in the oven, Martha!"

"Oh!" Martha kicked at the dust ruffle of her bed. "I ate a few pieces of Halloween candy and I guess I just wasn't thinking about dinner. I'm sorry, Mom."

"Oh, Martha." Her mother looked around the room as she sat down on the unmade bed. "I really wish you'd pick up in here. Just a little bit each day," she said softly. Then she removed her sensible shoes and lay down with a sigh, closing her eyes.

"How about if we put the casserole in the oven at 450 degrees instead of 350?" suggested Martha. "Then everything will cook faster, won't it?"

Her mother opened her eyes and smiled. "No, then it'll be burnt on top and raw in the middle. We'll just have to open up a can of tuna and make a salad." She glanced at her watch. "It's 6:03. Your father will walk in the door in two minutes, hungry and grumpy as a bear."

Which he did, at 6:05, right on the dot.

"We're in here, Bernard," called Mrs. Green, and Mr. Green, looking hungry and grumpy, found them in the bedroom.

"How was your day?" asked Martha's mother.

"The same," he said, loosening his tie.

Martha noticed the tired lines on her father's face. Sometimes, guiltily, she wished for a different kind of father. A father like the tennis-playing dads in cereal commercials, cheerful and suntanned and full of pep.

"We have a bit of bad news, hon," said Mrs. Green.

Martha's father slowly put down his heavy briefcase. He waited for the bad news, an anxious look on his face.

"Oh, it's nothing serious, Bernard!" said her mother quickly. "Except that we have to eat a cold tuna fish salad tonight. Martha forgot to heat up our dinner."

Martha's father sat down on her bed. "Tuna?" he asked, a scowl on his face. "Tuna?" he repeated. "I almost had a heart attack just now, thinking that something terrible had happened, and you're telling me that the bad news is tuna?"

Oh, dear, thought Martha, her stomach feeling tight and troubled, as it always did when her parents argued. And this time it was all her fault.

"Dad, don't forget that tuna is *much* better than Mom's mushroom pot roast," Martha said. She glanced at her mother apologetically. "Better for your heart, I mean."

Her parents, frowning, turned to look at her. And suddenly a very surprising thing happened.

Martha's father began to laugh, loud and long. And her mother began to giggle. Martha, relieved, giggled, too. Her father leaned over to kiss Martha, then pulled Mrs. Green to her feet and began to waltz her around the room.

"I should be angry at you for scaring me like that," he said, "but how can I be angry when you look so enchanting?"

Martha's mother leaned her head on his shoulder. "You're not so bad-looking yourself, handsome," she murmured.

Martha scrutinized her parents carefully. It was true! At that moment, her serious dad and her frumpy mom looked very much like Martha's favorite old photo of them as a laughing bride and groom. She hadn't seen her parents this happy in a long, long time. She wished she could watch them dance forever.

Her father laughed again, romantically dipping and twirling her mother to a silent dance tune. But was the tune really silent? As she listened to the laughter and the shuffle of dancing feet, Martha was almost certain she heard the music of the E minor chord hovering in the air.

Now is a good time to show them the guitar, she thought.

But before she could do so, her father said, "I'm going out to get us some pizza."

Martha was entirely taken aback. Her parents had

always pointed out that purchased pizza cost as much as two nourishing casseroles that provided left-overs! But before Martha knew it, her father had returned with a pizza, king-size, with all the trimmings.

"Bernard, peppers, too? You know what they do to you," warned Mrs. Green.

"Tonight I eat peppers," said Martha's father. "Plenty of nights to eat tuna and pot roast. What's wrong with living it up every now and then?"

Martha happily dangled a long piece of stretchy cheese into her mouth. When she had finished one piece, she ate another. And then another. There were no leftovers at the end of the meal.

After dinner Mr. Green disappeared behind his newspaper. Mrs. Green settled down on the sofa for the family's nightly checkup telephone call to Grandpa Green.

Now! thought Martha. She ran to her bedroom.

"What's this?" exclaimed her mother, putting down the telephone receiver when she saw Martha lugging the giant carton into the room.

Martha pulled out the guitar, *The Guitar Player's Manual*, and the letter to Interested Party. "This came today. I forgot to mention it before," she said. Her parents couldn't help but be impressed by the guitar's handsome purple hue, looking even more lustrous in the glow of the living room lamp.

Mr. and Mrs. Green took turns reading the letter

and silently examining the guitar. Then they began to have a discussion, as if Martha were invisible.

"There should be a law," said Mrs. Green, clucking her tongue. "Is there, Bernard?"

"No," said Mr. Green. "Anyone can send cheap junk anywhere they want through the mail."

Cheap junk!

"Or else there was a computer error and it was delivered to the wrong party," her father continued.

"I think it's very pretty," said Martha.

"Oh, Martha!" exclaimed her mother, tapping the guitar with her fingernail. "Honey, it's nothing but a piece of plastic. Two hundred dollars for plastic! Can you imagine the nerve, Bernard?"

"One hundred and fifty dollars," corrected Martha. "Or ninety-nine ninety-nine down. With easy credit terms. But the best part is that it's absolutely free for six weeks while you learn how to play in six easy exercises."

"Typical come-on. It's worth about nine dollars," said Mr. Green, putting the guitar back into its case. Then he dropped letter, manual, and case into the carton. He got up from his easy chair and returned with a roll of masking tape and a fat, black marking pen. "It's just a racket, Marth! Nothing's free. First of all, nobody learns to play that quickly. So you end up paying the money and keeping the guitar when the six weeks are over. Then they try to get you to sign up for expensive lessons. Or maybe you decide to return the guitar. Next thing you know, they charge you a fortune for wear and tear, threaten to sue. You just can't win."

Mr. Green began to slap tape around the sides of the carton. "And credit's *never* easy, believe you me! Interest charges multiply quicker than fleas. Your mom will return this tomorrow."

A dark look had come over her father's face, a look Martha had seen before. A look she suspected had something to do with his business and money problems from long ago.

"I won't need extra lessons," said Martha in a small voice. But her parents weren't listening. They had begun to argue.

"Why must you always depend on *me* to drop everything and attend to things! I can't possibly get to the post office tomorrow!" her mother was saying.

Her father wrote RETURN TO SENDER in big, angry letters across the top of the box. "I've got a very busy day ahead of me!" he said, beginning to raise his voice.

"Don't you think *I* do?" demanded her mother, tears springing to her eyes. "Don't you think *my* work is as important as *your* work?"

"Oh, Vivien, not *that* again!" snapped her father.

Martha's stomach had begun to hurt. "I'll take it to the post office," she said. "I have time after school."

Her parents turned to look at her. "Of course," said Mrs. Green. "I didn't even think of that. Thanks, honey."

"Well, I'm glad that's settled," said Mr. Green, rubbing his chest and grimacing. "Those peppers!" He began to read his newspaper.

"I warned you, Bernard," said Mrs. Green, picking up the telephone receiver and beginning to dial.

Late that night when she could hear her parents snoring softly, Martha crept from her bedroom. In the darkness she tore the tape from around the box and reached in for the guitar and *The Guitar Player's Manual.*

"Chords have power, but beware!" she read by a window's moonlight. "Players often remember only their chords, and forget to remember their music."

What did that mean? She would never forget the music! Martha strummed the E minor chord again and listened with all her might. Its sad, sweet sound reminded her of the feeling she got when she wished for something very hard.

And all of a sudden Martha knew what she had to do.

Five

ON Halloween Martha dressed as a movie star at the Academy Awards, wearing her mother's red nightgown over her clothes and borrowing her father's old bowling trophy to use as an Academy Award.

"At least someone's getting use out of that flimsy nightgown," said her mother. "Whenever I wore it, I woke up in the morning with a cold."

Martha thought about the gorgeous mothers in shampoo commercials, brushing their shiny hair and the hair of their daughters, also gorgeous. Dressed in flimsy nightgowns for bed, *they* never seemed to worry about colds. She pretended she herself was gorgeous as she taped a paper pumpkin to the Greens' front door. She poured her half-bag of Halloween candy into a bowl, then sat down on the sofa, the bowl in her lap, to wait for trick-or-treaters.

She tried hard not to think about pumpkin bashes. But Martha knew from experience that when a person tried hard *not* to think about something, that very thing kept popping up in the person's imagination, which was just what happened. She wondered if pumpkins were actually *bashed* at a party like that. She hoped not. Most likely you just bobbed for apples, pinned tails on paper cats, admired everyone's costumes, and ate little cupcakes with orange and licorice icing.

"Oh, who cares?" Martha whispered.

She did, that was who. Just the other day, she'd decided to have a small party of her own. She'd even made a beautiful party invitation decorated with jolly pumpkins and terrified black cats and laughing old crones, very similar to Tiffany's invitations, in fact.

She had planned to share a wonderful secret at her party. This secret was so important, it could only be shared with a best friend, or best-friend-to-be. Hostesses telling secrets to special people at their own parties were rude, so Martha had decided to invite just one honored guest. Her invitation had read:

> DEAR JENNIFER,
> THESE WITCHES AND CATS DON'T EXAGGERATE
> ABOUT MY PARTY: PLEASE SAVE THE DATE!
> AFTER SCHOOL ON THE 31ST WE WILL DASH
> TO A VERY SMALL, MARVELOUS PUMPKIN BASH!

She had been late leaving for school. She had run all the way, not even minding the rain from a sudden shower, holding the invitation carefully under her sweater. All she had thought about was the fun they would have. And sharing her wonderful secret with Jennifer.

"You're late again, Martha," Miss Marshall had admonished her as Martha burst into the classroom, clutching the damp invitation. "And you look as if you swam here! What happened?"

Martha, wet sneakers squeaking, had sat down at her desk. And then she had seen it.

Perched against Jennifer Okuda's pink pencil case, unmistakable with its store-bought splash of Halloween colors, had been an invitation to Tiffany Oliver's pumpkin bash. "To J.O. from T.O." it had said, in big, black letters.

Martha had hung her head before anyone could see her eyes welling up with tears. "There was a flash flood on my street and it took a very long time to get across."

"Oh, Martha," Miss Marshall had said softly, raising her eyebrows. "No need to exaggerate."

Now Martha swallowed a piece of Halloween candy.

"Not a single trick-or-treater is coming to this apartment building!" she complained, loudly enough for her parents to hear as they sat drinking coffee in the kitchen. "Hordes of kids used to ring the doorbell when we lived in our old house!"

"I wouldn't say hordes exactly," called her father.

"Hordes," mumbled Martha, vaguely remembering the long-ago ringing of doorbells in happier days, by seemingly vast troops of costumed children. Halloween never came to Mariella Manor, where Martha's was the only pumpkin on the door.

"Why don't you and Winston trick-or-treat outside? You've enjoyed doing that with him in the past," said her mother.

Martha sighed. She rose from the sofa and went into the kitchen for a shopping bag.

"See you later," she said to her parents, then went upstairs to call on Winston.

"I'm not!" Martha heard Winston yell from inside his apartment. Then she heard his mom reply, "Oh yes you are, or you can't go!"

Martha rang the doorbell and Winston opened it, a dour expression on his face. He was wearing his beeping Volpa costume with a jacket over it. He smiled when he saw her.

"You came!" he cried. "Mom, I'm going out with Martha."

"Make sure Winston keeps his jacket on, Martha," called Winston's mother from the living room.

"She treats me like a baby," muttered Winston as they walked toward the elevator. He hurriedly rubbed away a tear, which Martha pretended not to notice. She knew that Winston was embarrassed to have his mom talk to her as if Martha were his babysitter.

"It *is* chilly out," she said.

"Not to me it isn't. Anyway, I can take the cold!"

declared Winston defiantly. "I can take more than she thinks." He looked down at his jacket. "How can I look menacing with a jacket on? It squashes the flames."

"It's only a Halloween costume, Win," said Martha.

Winston pulled off his jacket and stuffed it into his shopping bag. "*Only* a Halloween costume? It's only my favorite night of the entire year, that's all."

"Really? Why?"

Winston shrugged. "I don't know. Because of all the free candy, I guess." He reddened, then said softly, "That's not the only reason. It's because you can pretend to be someone else on Halloween. Hey, just for tonight, call me Volpa, okay?"

Martha nodded. She understood. Dressed as a movie star at the Academy Awards, she could pretend she was Mariella Emerald, star. She suddenly had a warm feeling toward Winston, for he had just told her a secret. She owed him one back.

"Call me Mariella," she said. "Mariella Emerald. It's a name I wish I had. And now, Volpa, I'm going to show you something special."

In the elevator, Martha pressed *P* for Parking.

"Why are we going down to the dungeon?" asked Winston.

"You'll see," said Martha, smiling a secretive smile.

She led the way through the subterranean parking level, lined with small storage rooms in which tenants kept belongings they didn't use often.

"It's creepy down here," Winston said, his beeping bicycle light and softly humming radios echoing in the cavernous parking area.

Martha stopped at storage room 302 and removed the keys hanging from a chain around her neck. A little silver one opened the wooden door.

Winston stood outside, peering in. A cobweb hung from a light bulb that had hardly brightened the shadows when Martha pulled the string. "I see spiders in there," he said.

"Oh, come on in, Volpa," said Martha. "They won't hurt you."

She lifted the plastic sheet protecting her old bicycle. Out from under her bike she pulled the big box and from the box, the guitar case. She took out the purple guitar. "Look what I've got!" she exclaimed.

"Wow!" said Winston, stepping inside the room. "But why are you keeping it way down here?"

Martha stroked the guitar. "It doesn't really belong to me."

"You mean you *stole* it?"

Martha hesitated. "My parents said they didn't want to keep it. I was supposed to return it, but I didn't. Don't you dare tell."

Then she showed Winston *The Guitar Player's Manual*, promising to help her delight and amaze her friends and family in six easy exercises based on the five human senses.

"I've already finished two exercises, so I'm one week ahead of schedule. Listen!"

Martha strummed her E minor chord. Its song filled the dark corners of the damp and musty room.

"You're very good," said Winston.

"I know," said Martha proudly. "I've been practicing all week, whenever I can. Before and after school."

Winston crouched down to leaf through the manual. He read:

> EXERCISE NUMBER THREE: *The Sense of Taste*. Performance requires both *energy* and *courage*. (a) Too much sugar in the system saps energy. Eat healthfully. (b) The more you play for others, the braver you will feel, "For courage mounteth with occasion." It may be helpful to perform with a friend from time to time. Thus will you taste success and reap reward, Guitar Player!

"What kind of guitar lesson is that?" asked Winston.

"I really don't know."

" 'For courage mounteth with occasion.' That's Shakespeare, *King John*, act 2. We're reading him at the Hollyhock Academy."

"But I don't know any other guitar players to perform with," said Martha worriedly.

Winston jumped up. "Who says it has to be a guitar? I can play my clarinet! Marth, think of all the rewards we can reap if we play together while we're trick-or-treating. What a terrific idea!"

"But you hate your clarinet with a passion," Martha reminded him.

"Actually, I really like it," Winston admitted sheepishly. "I just hate to practice under pressure. I'll go right upstairs to get it."

Holding her guitar, Martha waited for Winston in the lobby. He returned very soon.

"I told my mom my radios were itching me and I wanted to leave them at home," he said. Then he pulled his clarinet from its hiding place in his candy bag. "Let's practice before we start out. Whenever I nod my head, you play your chord."

Winston tooted and Martha strummed. At first Winston's head nods directed her, but soon Martha's very own ear told her when to play her chord. The music swelled, echoing in the lobby, traveling down the halls and floating under doors. A woman from 101 and a man from 104 poked their heads out their doorways. A young man from 110 emerged, snapping his fingers. Humming to the music, a couple from 107 waltzed into the lobby, followed by their little boy, dancing in his bathrobe. Before Martha knew it, they were reaping rewards of candy and spare change from many of the first-floor tenants of Mariella Manor, most of whom Martha had never met, certainly not on any Halloween she could remember.

The crabby young man from 308 was coming in from the street. He stopped to listen. "Hmm," he murmured, when Martha and Winston had completed their performance to the applause of the first floor tenants. "Interesting. A bit of Brahms' Symphony Number Four in E Minor, eh?"

"Right," said Winston.

Up until then Martha hadn't realized she had been playing something as fancy as Brahms! She beamed with pride.

The tenant from 308 held out his hand. "Oscar Romanoff, here. Pleased to meet you. You make wonderful music."

"Volpa," said Winston, shaking Mr. Romanoff's hand.

Martha held back her laughter. "Mariella Emerald," she blurted out, inspired by Winston's response. "We've met before."

The man from 308 narrowed his eyes. "Ah, yes," he said. "I remember now. In the elevator. I was quite snappish with you, wasn't I? Please accept my apologies. I was running late at the time." He stepped back to get a better look at Martha. "But you have such an enchanting presence this evening, Mariella, I hardly recognized you."

An enchanting presence! Martha wasn't sure what *presence* meant exactly, but coming from stylish Mr. Romanoff, it sounded intriguing. She imagined it was like the difference between a gray sky and a sunrise.

Or maybe a plastic whistle and Winston's clarinet. Or between a plain glass of water and a nice, bubbly glass of seltzer!

Other tenants introduced themselves, then returned cheerfully to their apartments. Martha tore a small section from the top of her candy bag and crossed the lobby to the suggestion box. "I suggest," she wrote with the pencil stub hanging from the string, "that the lobby be decorated and Mariella Manor bashes be held on all major holidays." She signed it, "A Tenant, Martha Green."

As Martha and Winston were about to leave the building, the woman from 101 called out to them. "My name is Mrs. Perez," she said, an anxious expression on her face. "Would you two kids please do me a favor? My husband is out of town, and my son, Joseph, has a fever. I need to go to the pharmacy to get some medicine. I'll only be a few minutes."

Martha and Winston agreed to baby-sit, and Mrs. Perez quickly slipped on her coat and left them with the baby. Joseph was whimpering in his crib.

"I better not get too close in case he's contagious," said Winston, frowning. He stood by the door to the baby's room.

Martha picked up baby Joseph very carefully, like a bag of groceries with the eggs placed on top. She held the back of his small, fuzzy head to support his wobbly neck. His head felt hot. Martha remembered what it felt like to have a fever, when it hurt just to open her eyes and her head beat as if it had a drum inside of it. Her own head hurt, just remembering. Joseph cried and cried, as if he were trying to tell them something, which of course he was. Martha wished she could help him.

She laid the baby down and picked up her guitar. Very, very softly, as if she were stroking a feather across its strings, Martha strummed her chord. Immediately, Joseph turned his head toward her. He began to listen to the E minor chord instead of the drum inside his head. To Martha's joy, he closed his eyes and soon was fast asleep.

"Thank you, thank you!" cried Mrs. Perez when she returned. She handed Martha and Winston each a five dollar bill. "For Halloween. And because you earned it."

Martha shivered as they stepped outside, partly from the chill of the dark October night, but partly because of a small thought that was forming in her mind, a small, happy, astounding thought about her guitar. The thought kept growing, like a shooting star coming closer and closer.

Six

WINSTON pulled his jacket from his candy bag.

"How come my mom is always right? How did she know for sure I'd be cold?" he muttered.

"Oh, come on, Volpa," said Martha. "Everybody knows that this city is really a desert. Warm during the day and cool at night, when the sun goes down. You know that, too."

"I guess." Winston put on the jacket hurriedly. "But my mother thinks she knows everything about me, and most of the time she's right! I can't keep any secrets from her. Boy, if *I* had a guitar hidden in our storage room, she'd sniff it out in a minute. It's as if she can read my mind. She even knows how scared I am all the time." Winston's voice cracked a little. "Now *you* know, too."

"Everybody gets scared," said Martha. It was *not* a surprise to her that Winston was scared, only that he thought she didn't know.

"But I'm scared of thirty-three things and the list

keeps growing." Winston began to count on his fingers. "Anteaters, avalanches, bugs, cobras, darkness, dying, earthquakes, fire, gorillas, hit men—" He broke off suddenly. "You probably don't want to hear the whole list."

"What do you have for Y, just out of curiosity?"

"Yaks."

Martha giggled. "I hate to tell you this, but I saw a herd of them galloping down the boulevard the other day."

Winston frowned. "It's statistically possible, you know. A yak could escape from the zoo, for instance. Aw, now you think I'm weird."

"I'm sorry, Win—I mean, Volpa. I shouldn't have joked about it. I'm afraid of cobras, too. And dying and gorillas and probably lots of other things."

They were walking past the other buildings on their street, Cynthia Corners and Gloria Gardens. Martha assumed that Cynthia and Gloria were the landlord's other daughters. She liked to imagine that Mariella was the youngest daughter, the most beautiful and talented one, the one Mariella's parents loved the most.

"And I'm afraid that I could keep all the secrets in the whole wide world from my parents, and they wouldn't even notice," she said softly.

Suddenly Martha was filled with excitement, remembering her astounding thought of a few moments ago. "But in only three more exercises, everything will be different! Everything! And then they'll know!"

"Know what?"

She looked at Winston askance, surprised he'd forgotten. "That I can play the guitar, of course. And that I can delight and amaze." Martha stopped walking and leaned toward Winston. "And remember I told you about Mrs. Fifer in the supermarket, the lady with the fruit on her hat who discovered me long ago? Remember Souper Soup?"

Winston slurped at an imaginary spoon. "This soup's soo-per!" he shouted. "How could I forget? What about it?"

"Volpa, it's going to happen again. I'm going to be discovered a second time. I'm going to be a *star* called Mariella Emerald!"

Winston gave a long, low whistle. "Wow," he said. "You've got high hopes."

Martha hesitated. She just *had* to tell somebody. "It's more than high hopes," she said, her voice trembling. "I *know* it will happen. Because with this guitar *anything* can happen."

There. She'd said it out loud. She glanced sideways at Winston to see the effect on him. He had a kind, but worried, look on his face.

"You do play it very well," he said. "It's hard to tell at this point, with only one chord, but you do sound like you're on your way, Marth."

Martha put a hand on his arm and squeezed gently. "You don't understand. Volpa, I'm beginning to think this guitar has special powers."

"Special powers?"

"*You* know. Magic. Luck. That sort of thing."

Winston snorted, then looked at Martha apologetically. "I'm sorry. Marth, it's a nice guitar. And as I said, you *do* play it very well. But why do you think it's special? I thought you didn't like science fiction."

Martha frowned and held the guitar close. "It's not fiction! Because ever since it appeared on my doorstep, just like that"—Martha snapped her fingers—"I've noticed that good things have happened. For instance, when its music is in the air, my parents act romantic, people shower us with candy and money and tell us their names, babies stop crying. And when I play it, I've got presence! You have to admit those are all good things."

Winston shrugged, looking unconvinced. "Let me ask you a question," he said. "After you learn to play this lucky guitar, after the six lessons are over, how are you going to pay for it? Ninety-nine dollars and ninety-nine cents is a lot of money."

Martha didn't answer.

"And what if they start to send angry letters and bills to your house?" continued Winston. "What if they phone day and night to get their merchandise back. Then what?"

Martha angrily turned to face him. "For someone

who goes to the Hollyhock Academy for the Highly Gifted, sometimes you surprise me. By the end of the six weeks, because of this guitar, the good things will have happened already! So it'll all work out, don't you see?"

She stomped up the walk of a house with a picket fence, shutters, and a lit-up pumpkin in the window, just the kind of cozy house she wished she lived in. A little girl in a witch's costume patiently listened while Martha and Winston strummed and tooted and then gave each a prepared bag of candy. In the house next door, a man wearing a Batman mask shouted "Bravo!" and dropped gumdrops and lollipops into their bags.

"See?" said Martha triumphantly as they continued down the block.

"See what?" exclaimed Winston, looking exasperated. "They're giving everybody candy."

Martha pretended not to hear, staring stonily ahead.

"Well, if you're going to be mad at me just for expressing my opinion, I'm going home!" cried Winston. "I'm getting kind of tired, anyway."

Martha glanced at Winston. His face *did* look tired and pale in the moonlight. Suddenly she felt guilty. Even though it probably wasn't Winston's last Halloween, *he* might think it was. Now she was upsetting him.

"Of course you can express your opinion, Volpa," said Martha. "Just as I can express mine. If I choose to believe in the supernatural, that's my business. I was just hoping you'd agree, that's all."

"Well, I was just worried about the logical consequences of your actions."

Martha smiled. "Logic is your middle name, Volpa L. Hooper. But thanks for caring about me. And I'm not really mad at you."

They turned toward home. The streets were quiet, except for an occasional passing car, the whoop of a late trick-or-treater in the distance, and the soft beeps of Winston's Volpa headdress. Then, as they hurried by the unlit alley between Gloria Gardens and Cynthia Corners, Martha heard a loud shout.

"Hey, kids!"

She turned to look. The voice belonged to a tall, skinny boy about high-school age who jumped out of the darkness and blocked their way.

"Whatta ya got there, kids?" said the boy in a rough voice.

"Looks like they've done our trick-or-treating for us, Web," said another teenage boy behind him. "Come on, guys, hand over the candy, and any dough you've got!"

"Well, well," said Web. "Look what else they've got! Man, we got lucky tonight, Cal."

"A gee-tar and a horn! Some treat!" Cal had mean eyes and a T-shirt that said OBEY OR DIE!

Martha and Winston stood frozen to the spot. Martha held her guitar as tightly as she could.

"Come on! Can't you hear? Can't you read?" Cal pointed to his T-shirt.

"My clarinet is very expensive," said Winston in a shaky voice.

"Good!" said Web. "Like my friend here said, hand everything over, kids."

Suddenly Martha strummed her chord. She strummed it so hard that she scraped her fingers. And as soon as she did that, Winston dropped his candy bag, put his clarinet to his lips, and blew an ear-splitting note so forcefully that the veins stood out on his neck. Web and Cal looked startled.

"Leave us alone, you big bullies!" Martha yelled. "Come on, Volpa, let's go!"

Winston stopped screeching his clarinet. He began to run, waving his clarinet like a sword. Martha ran behind him as fast as she could, her guitar bumping against her knees.

"Are they behind us?" Winston said, panting.

"No time to look," said Martha.

When they reached Mariella Manor, Winston quickly opened the door with his key. They raced inside. Martha slammed the door behind them, then turned to peer through the glass.

"They're not there," she said.

Winston didn't answer. He was leaning against the wall, breathing heavily.

"Winston!" cried Martha. She put her arm around him and led him to a couch in the lobby. He lay down and closed his eyes.

"Do you want me to get your mom?"

"No, no. I'll be all right," Winston whispered, then opened his eyes and sat up, waving his fist at the door. " 'We must awake endeavour for defence; For courage mounteth with occasion'!" Winston turned to Martha, an astonished look on his face. "Shakespeare and *The Guitar Player's Manual* were right, Marth," he said. "At first I was scared, terrified actually, but then when we figured out what to do, I wasn't scared anymore."

"I know," said Martha. "It showed."

Winston beamed. "I feel much better. This was the best Halloween of my entire life."

"It *was* a pretty good one," agreed Martha, realizing she hadn't thought about Tiffany's pumpkin bash for hours.

"Except for the fact that those—those Halloween marauders took my candy!" exclaimed Winston indignantly.

"Here, have mine." Martha handed him her bag. "I need to stop eating candy, anyhow."

Downstairs in the storage room, Martha removed her guitar. Its purple plastic gleamed in the amber light.

Winston took it from her. Silently, he peered into the dark sound hole, then rubbed his hand carefully over the instrument's smooth, curved surface.

"Martha, look at this," he said.

Etched in golden, fancy script on the back of the guitar were two tiny initials.

"M.E." Winston read. "For Musical Enterprises."

"No!" said Martha. The tip of her finger touched each golden letter, one at a time. "No," she whispered, shivering with the rightness of it. "M.E. is for Mariella Emerald."

Seven

FINDING the golden initials of Mariella Emerald engraved upon the guitar filled Martha with an exhilaration she couldn't remember feeling since she had been a Souper Soup and a Wendy Wet child, so long ago. Something wonderful was meant to be. Oh, how certain she was about this, as certain as she was that the California sun would continue shining! Her discovery was around the corner. She just knew it.

Martha didn't hurry through Exercise Number Three, as she had done with Exercise Number One. She spent the entire week, before and after school, performing Brahms' Symphony Number Four in E Minor with Winston, or savoring the moment alone, strumming her chord.

One morning she was late for school again, having strummed and daydreamed a little too long in the storage room of the underground garage. Miss Marshall was already writing the day's vocabulary list on the chalkboard at the front of the room.

"Another flash flood, Martha?" asked Miss Marshall as Martha rushed by her.

Martha shook her head. "I just had a late start, that's all."

"Martha, there is no good excuse for a late start. You've been late too many times. I will have to telephone your parents about this."

Martha hesitated for a moment, then blurted out, "I was having a morning music lesson." *That* was a good excuse, she thought. And it wasn't really untrue.

Her teacher frowned. "Really? I didn't know you played an instrument."

"Oh, yes!" Martha exclaimed. "I take guitar. My teacher's name is Ms. Manual. Next time I'll set an alarm clock to remind us both when the lesson time is up."

Miss Marshall's frown deepened and she folded her arms in front of her. "Ms. Manual is scheduling your lesson at a very inconvenient time. I will still have to contact your parents."

"Oh, you don't have to do that! We'll change my lesson time to after school right away," Martha quickly assured her. She could hear her heart pounding in her ears. How she wished she hadn't brought up the guitar! "I'll never be late again."

"Good," said Miss Marshall, turning back to the chalkboard. "And how lucky you are to play an instrument."

"Yes," whispered Martha, filled with relief. She hurried to her seat.

Rochelle Ferguson, who sat beside Martha, pointed across the room.

"Look," she said. "They're all wearing yellow today."

Martha stared at the popular girls in their yellow ribbons, yellow socks, yellow sweaters, and yellow scarves. They looked like a charming bouquet of whispering daffodils as they clustered together by the pencil sharpener. They made everyone else look so drab in comparison. Oh, how Martha longed to be a part of that bouquet!

"I was sure it would be another color," mumbled Rochelle, who was wearing a green skirt and a green blouse. She stared at a piece of paper in her hand. "It was yellow only two days ago," she said. "I'm keeping track."

Poor Rochelle, thought Martha, although she, too, hadn't expected yellow again so soon. She imagined herself as Mariella Emerald, star, peeking out the window of a Cadillac limousine to see what color the popular girls were wearing that day. Then she would select an outfit from the rainbow of clothing hanging up inside the Cadillac, big as a room.

Martha giggled. Silly! When she was discovered, she'd *be* a popular girl. She'd know what to wear ahead of time.

"What's so funny?" asked Rochelle in a loud, angry

whisper. She crumpled up her piece of paper and threw it inside her desk. "I don't really care what they're wearing, you know. I just wanted to see if I could guess correctly."

"Oh, I'm not laughing at you, Rochelle," said Martha. "I was just thinking about something amusing Ms. Manual, my guitar teacher, said."

"Like what, for instance?"

"Well," Martha raised her voice slightly for the benefit of the canary-scarved Tiffany Oliver and the honey-ribboned Jennifer Okuda, who were returning to their seats, "see these red marks on my fingertips?" Martha held up her fingers for Rochelle, and anyone else, to see. "Everyone who plays the guitar a lot gets them. And you'll never guess what Ms. Manual calls them!"

"Calluses?" guessed Rochelle.

"Battle scars!"

Tiffany leaned over from her seat, surveying Martha's fingertips with a keen, interested look. "You could get those calluses from typing."

"On the thumb, too?" demanded Martha, wriggling her right thumb at Tiffany triumphantly.

"My brother plays the guitar, T.O., and his thumb has a red mark just like hers," Jennifer said.

Miss Marshall turned around, her chalk poised warningly. "Girls!" she said.

Martha quickly bent to her work, pleased,

though, to be lumped for a brief moment with T.O. and J.O.

I'll show them, she thought. When all of the exercises are completed and I've changed from plain old Martha Green to Mariella Emerald, I'll show them all.

Actually, she was already changing. In a Cinderella movie she had once seen, the fairy godmother waved her wand, the music swelled, and lovely silver sprinkles rained down upon Cinderella. Martha didn't see silver sprinkles, but she did hear the music. An E minor blast of a car horn. Little E minor chirps of the sparrows at dawn. The E minor hum of the clothes dryer. And other chords, too, everywhere, although she didn't know their names.

All week long she had been trying to eat healthfully, as the manual suggested. Except for three pieces of red licorice that happened to be lying in her desk drawer and a few lint-speckled chocolate raisins that she found in her pocket on the way home from school, Martha no longer ate candy. And everything else she ate had suddenly acquired a rich, inviting taste, including her mother's seven predictable casseroles.

Now when she entered the storage room of the underground garage, it seemed to Martha that even in the pitch dark she could see the shimmering gleam of the guitar case. And when she stood very still and hardly breathed, she seemed to hear faint, musical ripples in the air. She mentioned these strange but marvelous things to Winston.

"The pupil of the human eye adjusts to the darkness, opening wider to allow in more light," said Winston matter-of-factly. "And what you're hearing are the sounds of Mariella Manor's plumbing, that's all. Nothing magical about any of that."

"I guess not," said Martha wistfully. But she didn't really believe there was a perfectly logical, satisfactory explanation for everything.

Martha pulled the string dangling from the light bulb and turned to face Winston. Didn't he notice that he was changing, too? How much more cheerful he was lately! He wore his Volpa outfit proudly, whenever he pleased. He hardly ever talked about his heart operation, which was coming up, and he had recently mentioned that his list of thirty-three fears had shrunk to twenty-four.

"Hi there, little arachnid," said Winston to a spider hanging by its thread from a wooden beam. "*Pholcus phalangioides*, the cellar spider. An industrious little guy. Terrific web maker. And he's perfectly harmless. I just read up on him." Winston sat down on an old suitcase and began to fit the pieces of his clarinet together.

Martha flipped open her guitar case and shivered in anticipation as she pulled out the guitar and *The*

Guitar Player's Manual. It was time to forge ahead. She read out loud:

> EXERCISE NUMBER FOUR: *Strumming, Aerobics, and the Sense of Smell.* Congratulations, Guitar Player! You have reached the halfway mark, although we have much, much to do. We will begin the second half of your training with a study of *rhythm.* Footsteps and bird calls, raindrops and tennis games: Everything has a rhythm. We even carry our own tempo inside us, everywhere we go. You can hear it, if you listen. Take a moment to consider what that would be, Guitar Player.

Winston waved his hand impatiently. "Oh, easy," he said. "Heartbeats."

Martha tried to listen to her heart beating, with no success. But she certainly remembered its sound when Miss Marshall had threatened to call her parents. "I don't think that's the correct answer, Volpa. Can you hear your heart *all the time*?"

Winston nodded, his face solemn.

"Your poor heart, pumping so hard! That must be very difficult for you."

"It is." Winston hesitated. "Well, I don't really hear it all the time. Only when I get scared, especially when I think about my operation." He grimaced and turned away. "Darn! I was trying so hard not to complain anymore."

Martha put her hand on his shoulder. "That's okay."

"Really, I'm not as scared anymore."

"Don't worry, I know." She listened again. "Oh! The answer is breathing."

> If you guessed breathing, you are correct! Breathing is our natural rhythm. We breathe to live, and we live to breathe! Breathe the perfume of the rose; the rich, musky odor of a forest glen; and the salty fragrance of the ocean wave! Are you getting enough fresh air outdoors? Enough exercise? Many practitioners recommend aerobics as the exercise of choice.

"What does all that have to do with strumming?" muttered Martha impatiently. She had reached the halfway mark, but all she really knew how to do was play the E minor chord (lovely as it was) to Winston's Brahms.

" 'But we digress,' " she continued reading.

> Your new chord, the C chord, is a rather jaunty, smiling one. Finger it with your left hand, as in the picture on this page. Then, with your right hand, pick with your thumb and pluck with your fingers across the guitar face, as follows: pick-pluckety-pick. When you feel confident, strum the reverse:

pluck-pickety-pluck. *Do not hold your breath!* Breathe naturally and smell the world as you practice.

Beneath the instructions, the pretty hands of Ms. Manual demonstrated the new chord and strum. In another drawing, Ms. Manual, a whirl of computer-generated black dots, danced aerobically near a bed of roses.

Martha diligently tried to play the new chord with the pluckety-pick strum, but her fingers were as stiff as pencils and wouldn't obey. She tried repeatedly, until the tips of her fingers were sore.

"This is harder than the other exercises," she complained.

"Just keep at it, Marth."

She began again. Winston tooted a sprightly march on his clarinet, in perfect rhythm to Martha's slow and painful strumming.

Soon Martha put down the guitar and blew on her fingers. "It's no use. I just can't do it." Exasperated, she closed *The Guitar Player's Manual*, hard. It fell to the floor from its resting place on a suitcase.

"You can't expect to get it right away," said Winston, looking down at the manual on the floor. "You have to keep practicing."

"I hate practicing," mumbled Martha angrily, giving the manual a tiny kick with her foot. She looked up quickly, startled at herself. Why, here she was carrying on about practicing exactly the same way Winston did with his mom! "Imagine pretending the guitar is supernatural," she exclaimed. "If it *were* supernatural, then I wouldn't have to practice at all! It would just, just . . . happen!" Martha swept both arms up into the air, then down again, wriggling her fingers to imitate falling sprinkles. "I'm just a no-talent, big-baby exaggerator!" Martha had an empty, ashamed feeling in the pit of her stomach. She put her head in her arms and began to cry.

"Aw, Marth, please don't."

"My hopes are dashed. Completely dashed. I'll never be Mariella Emerald. Even *you* don't believe it. I call you Volpa, but you hardly ever call me Mariella." Martha could hear Winston pick up the manual from the floor and smooth its ruffled pages. She buried her head deeper in her arms.

"Funny thing about practicing," Winston was saying, his voice quiet and wondering. "If you *have* to do it—say your mom is nagging you and you do it so she'll stop—you may sound terrible. But one day you take your clarinet out on the roof. You hear music in your head so you face the sky and play. You sound wonderful! It's because of the practicing, but it's also because of the roof and the sky and the way you feel inside. I promise something like that will happen to you."

"Really?" asked Martha in a muffled voice.

Winston began to pace excitedly back and forth in the little room. "You can think of the practicing as a sort of catalyst in a chemistry experiment, making things happen! Like hydrogen is a catalyst for ferrous oxide!"

Martha lifted up her head to glare at him. "My guitar has nothing to do with chemistry experiments."

"I'm just making an *analogy*, Marth—I mean, Mariella!" Winston rolled his eyes to the ceiling, obviously frustrated. "And so what if I can't remember to call you by a different name?" he cried. "Don't you remember what the Bard said about the rose?"

"Who's the Bard?" asked Martha, blowing her nose into a crumpled tissue. She would look up *analogy* later.

"Shakespeare. In *Romeo and Juliet* he said—" Winston suddenly blushed. "Forget it. Shakespeare said lots of things. Let's go up on the roof to smell the world, like the manual says. And try again."

It did feel wonderful to be outdoors. Martha took a deep, satisfying breath, feeling the sunshine on her face. She pretended she was standing on a big stage, with the whole world her audience, spread out in front of her. The boulevard stretched like a ribbon from east to west to the ocean, bordered by tall palm trees and crowded with cars and Saturday shoppers. She heard the sharp shouts of children racing dirt bikes up and down the alley between Gloria Gardens and Cynthia Corners.

And down at the corner of her block she saw an old man walking slowly toward Mariella Manor. He was wearing a blue pajama top and carrying a cat.

"Oh, dear," said Martha. "It's Grandpa."

Eight

"GRANDPA, not again!" called Martha as loudly as she could from the roof.

Her grandfather looked up, startled. His eyes squinted into the sun.

"It's me, Martha! Stay right there. I'm coming." Leaving Winston, Martha raced down the back stairs to the street. "What happened this time?" she asked, hugging him.

"Ach, it's a long story," said Grandpa Green, sitting down on the curb to rest. Martha sat beside him and he leaned against her. His cat, whose name was Murray, snuggled comfortably between them. "On second thought, maybe it's not so long," said Grandpa Green. "I went out for a walk and here I am."

"But, Grandpa, in your pajama top?" cried Martha. She noticed that his collar had tea stains on it.

"What pajama top?" asked Grandpa Green indignantly. He looked down. "Oh."

"You were getting dressed and you forgot you were

getting dressed. Then you went outside to bring in the cat for breakfast and you forgot why you went out. So you decided to go for a walk and you forgot how to get back. Right?"

"I'm a busy man. I've got a lot on my mind." Her grandfather sighed, then grinned at Martha. "Such a smart girl. But I remembered the number two bus, didn't I? Brought me right here to see you."

"Oh, Grandpa," said Martha, putting her arm around him. "You've got to start paying more attention."

Winston came out of Mariella Manor, carrying the clarinet and guitar cases. "I didn't think it was a good idea to leave these lying around up there," he said to Martha.

"Grandpa, do you remember Winston? He lives upstairs from me."

"Of course I remember Winston," declared Grandpa Green, winking a greeting. "What do you think, I have a memory problem? Winston, the boy from upstairs. Winston, the musical prodigy who plays two instruments, yet."

"Winston is very talented," murmured Martha.

"Oh, boy, you kids today," said Grandpa Green. "All day long you play your loud music on the beach. Such terrific talent, right outside my window!"

Grandpa put his gnarled, blue-veined hands to his ears and made a face.

Martha and Winston looked at each other. Martha

knew they were both thinking the same thing. Music on the beach! Smell "the salty fragrance of the ocean wave," *The Guitar Player's Manual* had said. And here was Grandpa Green, come to remind them.

"Grandpa, we've got to get you home right away, before anyone sees you! Or else you-know-what may happen."

Martha ran up to her apartment to get a can of juice for her grandfather. She hid it from her parents and avoided telling them where she was going. Before long she, Winston, Grandpa Green, and Murray were sitting on the number two bus, on their way to Grandpa's little house.

"By the way, what's you-know-what?" asked Winston. They had gotten off the bus at Ocean Avenue and were walking toward Sandy Way, where Grandpa lived.

"Ah, Fenston, that's a long story," said Grandpa Green, reaching into his pocket for his jangling keys.

"Winston," Winston corrected him.

Smiling apologetically, Grandpa hit the side of his head with his hand. "Of course. Winston." He unlocked his front door, and Murray scampered into the house for his breakfast.

Inside, newspapers and books were scattered everywhere. Murray's dry food was spilled across the kitchen floor. Dirty plates and tea cups were piled on the kitchen counter, and Martha smelled burnt toast and sour milk.

"Then again," murmured Grandpa, "maybe it's not such a long story. You get old, you get tired, you forget things, and they cart you away to the you-know-what."

"Oh, Grandpa!" exclaimed Martha. "You're messier than I am." She poured a carton of old milk down the sink.

Winston leaned the clarinet and guitar cases against an overfilled bookcase. "You sure do a lot of reading," he remarked, looking around.

Grandpa removed some books from a chair and sat down with a sigh.

"Once I had pep. I'd do more than read. I'd discuss, I'd yell, I'd organize. Once I was a firebrand! A regular revolutionary!"

"I hear my parents talking on the phone to their friends and to my sisters," said Martha, squirting soap over the dishes in the sink. "They say that Grandpa is losing his memory and can't take care of himself well enough. They want to send him to a senior citizen apartment-hotel."

"Some hotel! A jail is more like it!" exclaimed Grandpa Green. "Some citizen! I ask you, Fenston, what kind of citizen gets carted away against his will?"

"Winston," said Winston softly.

But Grandpa didn't answer. The room was quiet, except for the sound of Martha running water in the kitchen sink. "I *am* losing my memory," said Grandpa Green after a while.

"But, Grandpa," said Martha, "you've just got to pay more attention. You've got a lot on your mind. You said so yourself."

Grandpa Green gave a tired sigh. "I've lost *all* my old stuff, I'm afraid, including my pep."

Martha plunged her hands into the warm, soapy water, afraid to turn around, afraid to see that maybe Grandpa was right. She rinsed her grandfather's dishes and placed them in a drainer by the sink to dry. Then she sat down at the kitchen table.

"If you would just clean up each time you dirtied something, a little bit each day, it wouldn't seem like such a big job, Grandpa," she said, taking his hand.

Grandpa Green shrugged. "Ach, it's only Murray and myself. Two old men." He leaned over to scratch under Murray's chin. "And Murray's not complaining." Then he smiled at Martha and Winston. "If I'd known I was going to have guests . . . but how was I to know? With music, yet!" He gestured to the instruments with his thumb. "So, Fenston, how about a concert to brighten up an old man's day?"

"Martha plays, too," said Winston.

Martha gave him a quick, warning glance.

"No kidding?" exclaimed Grandpa Green proudly.

"Yes, but it's a secret, Grandpa," said Martha, winking their special wink, which meant it was just between the two of them. "I want to surprise everybody when I'm ready."

Grandpa nodded, winking back.

Martha and Winston performed a bit of Brahms, and Grandpa applauded loudly. Then Grandpa himself sang a little song. Its words were in Yiddish, which Martha didn't understand. But its tune reminded her of the smell of soup simmering, the touch of a blanket, and the sound of the wind in the trees.

"That was the lullaby my mother used to sing to me," said Grandpa. He began to sing it again. Winston picked up the tune with his clarinet. Martha strummed her sad, sweet chord and her new jaunty, smiling one.

When he finished singing, Grandpa Green began to tell stories. He told how he left Germany as a Greenburger on a windy day in March, nineteen hundred and twenty-one, and how the U.S. immigration man, a Mr. Griffith, chopped off part of his name by mistake.

He told about working in a factory, making men's coats, and how the sewing machines screeched so loudly that the buzzing in his ears ("like mosquitoes!") continued even after he went home.

He told how he and his late best friend, Murray Fenston, would make speeches to hundreds of people who didn't have jobs or sufficient wages to properly feed their families. How he and Murray would paint signs that said ORGANIZE, and how once they were even arrested.

And finally he told about meeting Grandma Sophie on a sunny May 31, nineteen hundred and thirty-three. "She was wearing a funny straw hat the first time I saw her," Grandpa remembered. "What a beauty!"

Then he asked Martha and Winston to play his tune again, but faster this time. Grandpa began to dance spryly around the kitchen chairs. So did Murray, weaving in and out between Grandpa's legs. Martha had never seen a cat dance before. Then again, she had never seen her grandfather dance before. Martha and Winston followed Grandpa Green and his cat, around and around the chairs. And as she strummed and danced, Martha realized something wonderful. The magic had been released, just as Winston had promised. She was pick-pluckety-picking very well.

She also realized something else.

"Grandpa! You remember the words to old songs. You remember dates, and when the wind blew and the sun shone. You remember people's names from long ago."

Grandpa Green flopped down onto a chair and wiped his forehead with his pajama sleeve. "Whew! I haven't danced like that since the old days. I was some dancer then. Sophie and I could sure shake a leg or two." He looked at Martha. "Maybe I *am* getting my old stuff back."

"And your memory!"

"Maybe so," said Grandpa. "Maybe so."

When it was nearing dusk and time to leave, Grandpa walked with them to the bus stop. Martha could hear radio music carried by the cool, salty ocean breeze.

"When Murray and I moved here thirty years ago, the beach was quiet and peaceful," said Grandpa. "A person could hear himself think."

"Murray is thirty years old? That's unusual longevity for a cat," commented Winston.

"Ah," said Grandpa. "That was the first Murray. *This* Murray is ten years old. I've had several cats since the first one, all Murrays. Except the females."

"Sophies," said Winston.

"You guessed it. A smart upstairs friend you've got there, Martha."

Martha and Winston promised Grandpa Green that they would return very soon with more songs. They said good-bye and watched him walk slowly toward Sandy Way.

"I'll bet you're his favorite grandchild," said Winston.

"Think so?" Martha had never before thought of herself as anyone's favorite. It was a lovely feeling. "How do you know?"

"You can just tell. Look how he acts."

"I've never seen him act this way. But you know what it is, Volpa. It's the magic of the music. Grandpa feels younger and you feel braver and I feel . . ." Martha wrapped her arms around herself and hugged. She felt happy, and lighter, somehow, as if by just breathing in the damp, salty air she had suddenly acquired the power to float away. "I feel like Mariella Emerald!"

Winston frowned.

Martha felt a sudden rush of anger toward him. In her mind's eye, she imagined a bunch of round, enchanted balloons slowly shriveling up to nothing, punctured by Winston's sharpness. But just because he was gifted didn't mean he was always right.

Nine

"DO you still think that guitar is numinous?" asked Winston one late afternoon as they were practicing Exercise Number Four in the underground storage room. The music seemed to envelop them both in a warm cocoon.

"Numinous?"

"Look it up." He smiled mischievously, annoyingly so.

But she did, and to her surprise, Martha liked what she found. *Numinous.* Filled with a sense of mystery. Numinous. A word that described the lovely sweetness of the guitar's music as it seemed to travel up, up from the storage room into every corner of Mariella Manor and beyond. Since she began to play, Martha noticed tenants calling greetings to one another and politely holding the elevator for those scurrying to catch it. She noticed pleasant, homey cooking odors wafting from doorways, including her own.

And inside her bedroom, a little bit each day,

fueled by a strange new happiness, Martha had begun to chuck out old papers and paraphernalia, sharpen pencils, match socks, and untangle marionettes. She'd pushed her neatly made bed against the wall to make room on the floor to play board games (Winston was teaching her chess), then swept up the mess lying beneath. She emptied the trash regularly.

"Keep up the good work," said her father. He still looked worried and tired, but every now and then Martha caught her mother kissing the top of his head as she went by, making him smile. And though they hadn't waltzed since the night of the pizza, one evening Mr. Green brought home a chrysanthemum plant—for absolutely no reason at all.

Numinous, numinous. Secretly, Martha examined herself in the mirror. She touched her face. She turned one way and then the other way, regarding herself out of the corner of her eye. And then one morning after her shower, surrounded by the soft, warm mist, her hair curling and her cheeks pink, Martha-in-the-mirror looked—yes!—almost adorable. With her finger Martha squeaked initials all over the steamy bathroom mirror: M.E.! M.E.!

"You look nice today," said Rosa Santiago, one of the popular girls, that morning at school.

Later Martha waited her turn by the drinking fountain, humming a tune. "How lucky to have an ear for music," said Jennifer Okuda, offering to share her cluster of grapes.

Numinous. One day the word touched Winston, too, as Martha and he sat on the number two bus for the beach.

"You know what my mom would make me do if she knew we were going to the beach?" he complained. "She'd make me slather up with sunscreen. Three inches thick. I'd have to wear this hat every single minute, even when I'm swimming."

Martha giggled. "You're exaggerating."

"Well, she *does* treat me like a baby. She just doesn't understand that I'm feeling stronger and stronger every single day." He clenched his fist and flexed his arm muscle. "Feel this. Doc says I'm tough as nails, inside and out. Tougher than I've ever been."

Martha reached out to touch his arm. "Tough as nails," she agreed.

Winston flipped open his clarinet case, then removed his hat and dropped it inside. "Know something? I don't even think I need any old heart operation." He snapped his case shut with two emphatic clicks. "I think I'm cured."

"Winston!" cried Martha. "That's miraculous!"

Winston nodded slowly. "Numinously speaking, it is, isn't it? I feel great. I don't think I need an operation," he repeated, a hopeful look on his face.

When they reached the beach, their first stop was Sandy Way, where Grandpa Green was painting his front door red. Martha noticed that her grandfather was wearing the T-shirt her family had bought him for his last birthday. It said SENIOR POWER in big, bold letters.

"My good pal Murray Fenston used to say, 'A door with a new coat means welcome.' You kids go play. I've got work to do."

Martha and Winston walked down to the sand. They spread out the big towel Martha had brought and sat down on it. Then Martha opened *The Guitar Player's Manual.* She read aloud:

> EXERCISE NUMBER FIVE: *The Sense of Sight.* In order to sing songs, one must have pictures in one's mind. Take a look around you, Guitar Player. Go ahead: a good, hard look.

Martha took a good, hard look all around her. The waves were as green as emeralds and the white sand sparkled. Beach homes, lined up in the distance, were colored crayon bright. Sea gulls waddled everywhere, but there were hardly any people. To Martha's right was a silver garbage pail. Beyond the garbage pail, a man and a woman sat cross-legged on a blanket.

" 'You are ready for what comes next,' " she continued.

> You know a sad-sweet and a smiling chord and several lovely strums. Add to your knowledge two simple chords, G and D^7. Then, using all the senses you possess, you will know more than fifty songs.

Martha caught her breath. "More than fifty songs! Winston, that's impossible."

"No, it isn't," declared Winston, beginning to fit together the pieces of his clarinet. "Lots of songs can be played with only four chords. You'll see."

There were two drawings in which Ms. Manual demonstrated the new chords. Martha copied her, pressing each chord with her left hand while pickety-plucking with her right. In no time at all, she had learned the new music.

"Let's begin," said Winston.

First they played short, easy songs, songs Martha had enjoyed singing when she had been a very little girl, including her long-ago favorite, "Old Macdonald Had a Farm." They played an ocean song and a sun song and a song about birds. They played a song about waking and a song about sleeping, and songs about fighting and love. Some songs were sad-sweet. Martha sang those softly, curling her fingers gently over the guitar strings. Others made her giggle so much she couldn't get the words out, and Winston couldn't blow his clarinet for the smile on his face. Soon, by her count, they had played twenty-five.

"Hey, sister. Hey, brother." The young man sitting on the blanket was pulling something from a big case. The golden curves of a saxophone winked in the sunlight.

"Come jam with us," he said, putting the saxophone to his lips and blowing a clear, light note. His girlfriend waved at them and pulled a pair of bongo drums from a brightly striped bag.

Jam! Martha knew what that meant. That meant they would all play together, just like a group in a music video. Martha and Winston picked up their instruments and went over to join the man and woman.

"Bee-Bob," said the saxophone player, introducing himself. "And this here's Alula, the triple-great-granddaughter of African royalty."

Alula had long hair and skin the color of coffee with cream. On every single finger and some of her toes, she wore a ring. Bracelets, up and down her arms, jangled in time to the soft tapping on her bongo drums. She sat very straight, like a queen. Martha thought she was beautiful.

"Volpa," said Winston, shaking Bee-Bob's hand. "I've never jammed before."

"You play a mean horn," said Bee-Bob. "You'll do fine."

"Mariella Emerald," said Martha. "I'm just a beginner. I know three strums and four chords and I've only had five lessons."

"You're joking me!" exclaimed Bee-Bob, studying Martha over his dark sunglasses. "Then what was all that joyful singing and playing we heard over there? You play like an angel. Doesn't she, Alula?"

"At the pearly gates," said Alula, tapping softly on her bongo drums.

"Play what you know," said Bee-Bob. "My sax will follow."

Martha strummed and Winston tooted. Then, suddenly, Bee-Bob and Alula took Martha and Winston's melody and created something new. Ripples and trills and jazzy surprises tickled Martha's ears. Whenever Martha changed her chord, Bee-Bob's sax followed, just as he'd promised. Martha sat straight and proud, like Alula. She felt as if everything in the whole, wide world had come together in one beautiful song. Jamming was glorious.

A small crowd had formed around them, from nowhere it seemed, swaying to the music. Soon Bee-Bob blew one loud note, Alula hit her bongo drums hard and fast, and the song was over. The audience clapped, and to Martha's great surprise, a shower of coins and bills fell into Bee-Bob's open saxophone case.

"Thanks much," said Bee-Bob to the crowd. Alula bowed gracefully over her drums. After they had rolled up their blanket and put away their instruments, Alula counted up the money and gave three dollars each to Martha and Winston. Martha was thrilled. Her first earnings as a performer!

"Hope to play another gig with you guys real soon," said Bee-Bob, shaking their hands. Then he put his arm around the triple-great, regal Alula and they both strolled away toward the sun.

Martha and Winston gathered their things together

and went back to Grandpa Green's. He had already finished painting his front door and had started on the window frames. "Eat some cookies before you leave. They're on the kitchen table," he said. "Poppy seed. Sophie's recipe. A miracle, it suddenly came to me!"

On the bus for home Martha leaned her cheek against the cool window and sighed from deep inside of her.

"Oh, Win, wasn't it a numinously terrific day?"

Winston didn't answer. He was fast asleep, his nose bright pink from the sun.

Ten

THE November weeks were slipping by. The sixth-grade class spoke of pilgrims, and Miss Marshall hung up her festive paper turkey. Martha threw herself into her schoolwork so that her teacher would have no reason at all to complain to her parents, especially since she had told about the forbidden guitar.

One day, chosen by Miss Marshall to plan the Thanksgiving bulletin board, Martha and Jennifer Okuda worked as a team at a special table. Then they giggled together by the pencil sharpener until Tiffany pulled Jennifer away.

Oh, who cares? thought Martha. There was just no time to think about *them*, with their silly matched colors and private meetings in grand homes across the boulevard. She had much too much to keep her busy now. Perfecting fifty songs and playing chess with Winston. Homework. Helping Grandpa Green, who had recently decided to clean up his house—and not a minute too soon, either.

"Phew!" Martha muttered, her head in his refrigerator. She emerged, holding her nose with one hand and a piece of moldy cheese with the other. "This cheese is probably as old as Murray!" she exclaimed, to which Grandpa Green responded, "But *which* Murray, I wonder?"

On Thanksgiving Day, all of Mariella Manor smelled like one gigantic turkey. In the elevator Martha met several tenants going up. "Happy Thanksgiving," she said. "Happy Thanksgiving, Happy Thanksgiving," they murmured politely, to her and to one another.

Her own family, thought Martha, looking around the holiday table at her parents, her older sisters, Sabrina and Kimberly, and Grandpa Green, seemed just like that big, jolly family eating from shiny dishes in the television commercial for dishwashing detergent. She had never seen a fatter Thanksgiving turkey in her life. And the green beans had never been greener, or the sweet potatoes sweeter, and the tinkle of forks and knives on filled-up plates had never sounded merrier.

Of course things were always so much merrier when her older sisters came to dinner. Mr. and Mrs. Green asked Sabrina and Kimberly many questions, and they responded with tales about their interesting lives.

Sabrina talked about her advertising job and the cost of living and world affairs. Kimberly talked about college courses, term papers, and career options, as well as her boyfriend, who at that moment was digging up ancient, lost cities in a distant land. She passed his photo around the table and everybody agreed that he was very handsome.

Martha ate silently as the conversation flowed back and forth. How she longed to be part of the talk, with tales of her own to inspire proud gazes and interested questions.

"What *is* this?" asked Kimberly suddenly, holding up her fork with something dangling from the prongs.

Her mother leaned forward to take a closer look. "Steamed cactus."

"Mother, with *marshmallows*?" exclaimed Kimberly.

"The thought of the same old predictable Thanksgiving dinner was boring. We decided to add a southwestern touch to the meal," said Mrs. Green.

"*Très nouvelle*, Mom," said Sabrina, who had majored in French at college. "Smother anything with marshmallow and I'll eat it."

"The dish is inspired, Viv." Mr. Green looked proudly at his wife.

"Dad made the chili-dilly stuffing and Martha, the mystery bean salad," said Mrs. Green.

Kimberly wrinkled her nose and began to sort the cactus into a neat pile at the edge of her plate. "Well, I don't see what's wrong with your old Thanksgiving dishes. This is highly erratic behavior. What's gotten into you guys?"

Her mother sighed. "You were always such a picky eater, Kim," she said. "I'm not quite sure what's gotten into us, but it certainly is fun. And Martha tries everything."

Martha smiled down at her plate. It was as if the musical magic were everywhere, even heating up the kitchen stove and bubbling in the pots and pans. Kimberly, who was majoring in psychology, called it erratic, but Martha thought it was just plain terrific.

Suddenly Grandpa Green, silent until then, stood up as if he were going to make a speech. "I remember," he said, a faraway look in his eyes, "one Thanksgiving when we couldn't afford a turkey. Sophie put together a bird made out of Jell-O. Legs, wings, the whole thing."

"A Jell-O turkey!" cried Sabrina. "Oh, Grandpa, how pathetic!"

Grandpa Green looked around. "Pathetic? Why pathetic? Bernie, do you remember pathetic?"

"Those were lean years," said Martha's father.

"Lean, shmean," said Grandpa Green. "We were rich!"

"You're not remembering," said Martha's father quietly. "It was the depression. We were poor. Sit down and eat your dinner, Pop."

Grandpa Green continued standing. He stared down at his plate.

"Grandpa!" cried Martha, giving him their secret wink to warn him about you-know-what. She stood up and wagged her finger at him. "You do *so* remember! Tell them the date."

Grandpa Green thought for a few moments, then drew himself up tall, grinning at Martha. "November, nineteen hundred and thirty-eight."

"And you were wearing?"

"Gray pants, white shirt. Sophie, a green dress. Bernie, short pants. Your Aunt Anne, a nice blue blouse."

"Weather?"

Grandpa Green closed his eyes. "That's a toughy. Let's see: cloudy day, nippy wind; maybe fifty-five, sixty degrees." He opened his eyes and looked at Martha warmly. "See, I remember everything." He turned to his son and began talking in a stern voice, as if Martha's father were still a little boy wearing short pants. "We *were* rich," he said, his eyes flashing like a firebrand's. "We had each other. We had a lot of laughs: Nobody walked around with a long face. Every day was Thanksgiving, not just one day of the year."

Martha's father began to twirl a strand of marshmallow around his fork. He stared at it for a few moments, then looked up at his father and smiled. "You're right, Pop," he said. "I guess *I* wasn't remembering."

Grandpa Green sat down. He quickly stood up

again. "You know what else I remember?" Without waiting for an answer he picked up a spoon and pretended to slurp. Then he began to sing:

What do you say when you smell it?
What do you say when you taste it?
What do you say when you finish it up?

Grandpa paused to take a breath. Then he and Martha's mother and father and sisters shouted together, "This soup's soo-per!"

"You all remember!" cried Martha.

"Of course," said her father. "That company sold a lot of soup because of you."

"Gallons," said Sabrina.

Then everyone sang the Souper Soup song again. Martha felt very rich, thinking of Jell-O turkeys. She waved her genuine turkey leg in the air and began to sing, too, with all her might.

Eleven

LIKE the approach of a black, rumbling storm came the day-by-day realization that the six-week free trial was ending. Soon there was only one week, and one exercise left. What now? Martha thought, again and again.

"Congratulations, Guitar Player!" said Exercise Number Six. "You have reached the end, trained by our Marvelous Modern Method using the Five Human Senses. Now combine Exercises One through Five, and sing your song."

"But which song?" asked Martha. She and Winston were sitting on the couch in the lobby while Winston waited for his father to pick him up for dinner. "I know lots of songs. Counting the national anthem, I now know more than fifty!"

There were the twenty-five they had played that day at the beach, then five more from the jam session. Ten more she'd learned in the past week. Two she'd composed with Winston one rainy afternoon. And eight jingles she'd learned from television commercials, including Wendy Wet's and Souper Soup's.

Martha looked down at the book in her lap. She had reread the sixth exercise many times.

"It does seem incredibly simple," agreed Winston.

"And haven't I been singing all along? Songs about oceans and dogs and fried chicken and cars and anything else I can see, hear, touch, smell, and taste?"

On the last page of the manual was a sketch of the confident Ms. Manual. Her head was thrown back, her mouth open, and she was singing and playing with all her might. Martha bent down over the little book, half hoping she would hear snatches of Ms. Manual's apparently lively tune.

"It's a review exercise. That's why it's so easy. You can sing any song you like," said Winston, tugging uncomfortably at his tie. He was all dressed up for dinner at a fancy restaurant, his father having absolutely forbidden him to wear the Volpa outfit in his presence. "At Hollyhock, our instructors emphasize that if we learn the material well the first time, then the reviews will always be easy."

"Oh," said Martha, somewhat relieved. "I didn't think of that. Or maybe it's a reward for all the hard work I've done in One through Five. Like dessert."

A car horn honked. Winston jumped up from the couch to peer through the glass front door. He returned, downcast, looking at his watch. "It's not him. He's *always* late!" Then, brightening, he added, "Dad will be driving his new yellow sports car. Which I'm almost positive he'll let *me* drive as soon as I get my driver's license."

Martha smiled, glad for him, imagining a sixteen-year-old Winston zooming around the city in a yellow sports car. It was the first time she had ever heard Winston talk about the future.

"Before you know it," he continued, sitting down again, "I'll be picking you up after school. We'll comb the highways and byways and explore the whole waiting world."

"The Bard said that?"

"No, I did. Just now." He eagerly turned to face her. "Listen, I've been thinking. I've got over one hundred dollars in my savings account. It's yours. Just say the word."

Martha felt a rush of hope and gratitude run through her, then, just as quickly, a pang of disappointment.

"Doesn't your mother have to give her signed permission for you to withdraw it?"

"Well, yes, she does."

"Then you'd have to tell her everything. You said yourself she was hard to keep secrets from."

Winston nodded, a pained expression on his face.

"Thanks, anyway," said Martha. She looked down at the manual again. "Why would they even bother to congratulate me, if there wasn't something to look forward to?"

She closed her eyes and leaned her head against the couch. Suddenly, from far away, sending shivers up and down her spine, she heard a car horn (or a trumpet's call?) announce her name. She could have sworn she did. She opened her eyes and lifted up her head. "Mariella Emerald," she whispered hopefully. "Something will happen. I just know it."

Winston was silent. "Speaking of the Bard," he said after a while, "did I ever tell you what Shakespeare said about the rose?"

Martha slowly shook her head. "You started to, that day on the roof."

Winston studied the lobby rug. He took a deep breath, his cheeks reddening. "*Romeo and Juliet.* Act 2, scene 2. Romeo and Juliet are secretly in love. Juliet is leaning from her window, wishing their two families weren't feuding. She doesn't realize Romeo is eavesdropping. 'What's in a name?' Juliet asks. 'That which we call a rose, / By any other name would smell as sweet.'" Winston glanced up at Martha. "Shakespeare had a good point, you know."

Martha thought about it. "Humph," she said finally, shrugging her shoulders. "But I *like* the name Mariella Emerald!"

"You don't understand—" Winston started to say. But then a horn honked loudly and he ran to meet the sleek, yellow car pulling up to Mariella Manor.

Martha sat on the lobby couch for a long time,

trying hard not to think troublesome thoughts, wishing with all her heart that the free trial could last forever.

The following morning Miss Marshall demonstrated a fascinating science experiment. She wound wire around an ordinary iron nail, then connected the ends of the wire to a dry cell. When electricity flowed through the nail, it was transformed into a magnet, so that five little thumbtacks clung to the nail's magnetized tip.

The sixth-grade class bent over their experiment books, drawing diagrams of the transformed nail as Miss Marshall patrolled the rows. She stopped at Martha's desk. "Nice," she commented. "Your work habits have improved a great deal lately, I must say. How are the music lessons going?"

Pleased, Martha drew bright, red sparks around the magnetized nail tip. It was a careful, neat drawing.

"I know more than fifty songs," she said proudly. "No exaggeration."

"My goodness!" exclaimed her teacher. "Have you signed up for the Holiday Fest choir this year?"

Martha caught her breath. She had a much better idea! Why hadn't she thought of it before? Most students at Martha's school sang anonymously in the choir or, heavily made up and costumed, acted in plays. But only a few students performed solo. Last year Larry Brown had played "The Flight of the Bumblebee" on his trumpet faster (he said) than anyone on earth. And Martha would never, ever forget the girl who had danced on toe for ten whole exhilarating minutes, or the kindergartner who had juggled spoons. Or, most indelibly fixed in her memory, the lovely girl who had recited a very long poem and was later spotted in a Hollywood movie. Performing solo made you stand out forever in the lunchroom or the school yard or the hallway. But, most important, performing solo made you discoverable. This was it, of course, as it was meant to be. Her big chance to delight and amaze, just as *The Guitar Player's Manual* had predicted.

"I would like to sing a solo and accompany myself on my guitar," declared Martha to Miss Marshall, but looking straight at Tiffany Oliver, who looked back at her in surprise.

After school, Martha walked home behind the popular girls, who were all dressed in shades of purple. They looked just like a pretty bouquet of bluebells, violets, and lavender. Well, she wasn't even going to look their way. She would just think her own important thoughts and pass right by, as if they were invisible.

"Hey," called Tiffany as Martha, eyes averted, passed the group.

Martha turned. "What?" she asked defiantly.

"Are you really going to sing and play your guitar in the Holiday Fest?"

"Yes. Yes, I am." Martha stood stiffly, her two hands clenched at her sides, waiting to be called a name.

Tiffany approached her, smiling as if they were friends. "There could be directors or producers in the audience, you know, looking you over."

"I've thought the very same thing myself," said Martha.

"Directors and producers?" asked Jennifer. "Really?"

"Oh, yes." Tiffany nodded her head knowledgeably. Samantha Sampson, Courtney Morgenstern, and Rosa Santiago nodded their heads, too. "Don't forget, J.O., you live in Los Angeles now," Tiffany continued. "People are discovered here all the time. When we were in the third grade, a sixth-grade girl recited a poem ten verses long during the Holiday Fest. Then one day we saw her in a movie. We're all pretty sure it was the same person."

"Really!" exclaimed Jennifer.

Samantha glanced at Martha admiringly. "I'd be so nervous, up on a big stage by myself. Do you think you'll be nervous?"

"Yes," said Martha truthfully. Then she thought about Halloween night and that day at Grandpa Green's and jamming with Bee-Bob and Alula. She allowed herself one teensy-weensy charcoal-gray lie, and then another. "But I *have* performed before, you know. I call myself Mariella Emerald. That's why my guitar is monogrammed with the initials M.E."

"Monogrammed! Cool!" cried Tiffany. "And what a great name!"

"Great name!" chimed in Jennifer, Samantha, Courtney, and Rosa.

Oh, joy! Here she was, thought Martha, walking and having a discussion, quite naturally if you please, with the popular girls.

"What song are you going to sing on stage?" Tiffany asked.

"It's hard to choose," said Martha. "I'll have to think about it for a while."

Tiffany put her arm around Martha's shoulders and leaned her head close to Martha's. "When you've picked your song, sing it for us and we'll give you some tips. Then we'll help you choose your dress."

"Great idea, T.O.," said Courtney.

Tiffany looked pleased with herself. "It's settled, then. We'll be sort of like your managers."

Martha, not really sure what to say, felt as if she were riding on a train that was traveling a little too fast.

The girls had reached the boulevard. "Bye, Martha," said Samantha.

"Bye, *Mariella*," Tiffany corrected her.

Martha stood at the corner, watching them cross.

Suddenly, halfway across the busy street, Tiffany

turned and waved. "Hey, Mariella," she shouted. "We're all wearing orange tomorrow!"

During the next week, everything Martha had always longed for as she'd watched TV, admired other people, or sat dreaming alone in her bedroom, seemed to be coming true.

She pondered which of her fifty songs she would perform for the Holiday Fest. It would be a difficult decision. She had so many favorites. She would choose the most beautiful, the most glorious, the most numinous song she knew. She could almost hear the shower of applause. She could almost see the smiles of the audience and the proud looks of her parents, who would finally know what she could do. Then, "What a discovery you are, blessed with a musical magic!" someone would say. Someone with a big hat filled with plastic oranges and strawberries and—

"Marth, maybe nothing will happen that night," said Winston when she told him about the Holiday Fest.

"What do you mean?"

"I mean, I'm sure you'll do fine, but the odds are against discoveries, statistically speaking."

"Well, *I* think something *will* happen, Volpa L. Hooper. Look how much has happened already. And I'm not the only one who thinks so."

For at school, at least among Tiffany and her friends, she was Mariella Emerald, about to be discovered. A Mariella giggling in an orange cluster at the school-yard gate. A Mariella waiting in a green cluster by the pencil sharpener. A Mariella crossing the boulevard in a red cluster, on the way to do homework together after school.

There was a world beyond those clusters, yet for several days she hardly noticed. Sometimes she'd see a left-out Rochelle Ferguson, watching sadly. Then Grandpa Green phoned, wondering if she had the flu; he hadn't heard from her. One day, taped to the Mariella Manor mailboxes, there was an angry note: "WILL THE PERSON DYEING THEIR CLOTHING RED PLEASE NOT DO SO IN THE COMMUNAL WASHING MACHINE?!!! MY ENTIRE LAUNDRY TURNED PINK!!! O. ROMANOFF. APT. 308."

And then there was the thought, which she pushed away impatiently like an annoying insect, that the six-week free trial was over. The guitar wasn't hers any longer.

One afternoon after school, waiting on a corner, she saw Winston in his Volpa outfit, beeping lights and all.

"Look at that weirdo!" cried Tiffany. The other girls stopped talking to stare.

Winston began to wave. "Marth!" he called.

"Is he a *friend* of yours?" asked Tiffany.

"Oh," said Martha, glancing at Winston, then back again, ashamed because of what she was about to say. "He's just my upstairs neighbor."

"Better see what he wants. Maybe there's been a

fire," said Tiffany. The other girls giggled, then crossed the boulevard without her.

Winston met Martha halfway up the block and walked back home with her.

"You've been awfully busy the past few days," he said.

Martha nodded, feeling guilty, then angry at Winston for making her feel that way. She unlocked the lobby door and went to pick up the mail. With another guilty pang, she noticed that apartments 205, 207, 301, and 406 had added their complaints to Mr. Romanoff's. Who could have imagined that dyeing her sister Kimberly's little white skirt red would have such disastrous results throughout the entire building?

"Are those your new friends?"

"Um-hmm," replied Martha, distracted, for she had suddenly remembered that the group was going to wear stripes the next day. That would be a problem. The only striped clothing she owned was a pair of pajamas.

"Sort of a club? Where you all wear a uniform or something?"

"We're not a club and we're not wearing a uniform. We just like to dress alike, that's all. For fun."

Winston raised his eyebrows. "Conformity to the herd," he said, shaking his head. "Just as the theorists say."

Martha frowned as she reached into her mailbox for the letters inside. "What do you mean?"

"Conformity," repeated Winston. "At Hollyhock we're learning about the sociology of groups. When one joins a group, one conforms. Group pressure, you see. Very interesting stuff. And you probably know what the Bard said about all that, way ahead of his time. 'To thine own self be true,' et cetera."

"Oh, the Bard, Bard, Bard!" cried Martha, putting her hands over her ears. "Enough!" She pressed the elevator button hard, two times. "It isn't any of that stuff. It's just friendship, pure and simple."

"Friendship! Is that what *that* is, dressing in the same colors? Well, I think it's ridiculous."

"Yes, friendship! Don't they teach you about friendship at the Hollyhock Academy? At least *they* believe in me. And *you* think *I* look ridiculous? *You* think *I* do?"

The doors to the elevator opened. Martha stepped inside and turned to press 3. But Winston didn't follow. He stood very still, fingering his cape, his eyes squinting and his face pale.

"Winston! Are you okay?" asked Martha, suddenly alarmed.

"I'm fine," he answered coldly, removing his headdress.

"I didn't mean it," she quickly said, but Winston

was already walking away as the elevator doors closed between them.

"I really didn't mean it," Martha whispered to herself in the elevator mirror.

But he *did* look silly in his Volpa outfit. And he *was* a weirdo, with his theories and his Bard this and Bard that! Hang around someone like that and you become a weirdo, too, just the way you catch a cold. She stared at herself in the mirror, into her eyes, dark and not so nice, then looked away guiltily as the doors opened at the third floor. She would phone Winston and apologize right away.

Martha unlocked her apartment door and put the mail on the hall table. All at once she noticed the envelope on top of the pile. It looked official and important, festooned with colorful stamps. "Oh, no," she whispered.

It was a bill. She knew that immediately, for it had a little window in the envelope, as most bills do. Through the window Martha read, "To Resident, 1200 Forest Glen Drive, Apt. 302." At the top left-hand corner, the return address said Musical Enterprises, 1234 Tuneful Trail, Suite 10, Via del Mar, California. Martha tore it open.

"Our computer indicates," said a letter inside, "that on October 24 you received one purple guitar, Model ME123456. Please remit payment, or return the aforementioned merchandise."

Martha quickly folded up the bill and hid it in her

desk drawer. Then she dialed Winston's number to apologize and to tell him what had happened. She knew he was home because she could hear him practicing his clarinet. He did not answer the telephone.

That evening Martha could hardly eat her dinner, thinking about the bill, and her mother put a cool hand on her forehead to check for fever. At night Martha dreamed of a giant, angry computer spitting out hundreds and hundreds of purple envelopes with little windows on them. "BEWARE! BEWARE!" grumbled the computer. In the dream, the envelopes disappeared into thin air. But the next morning, the folded-up bill was right where she'd left it. Martha tore it into tiny pieces and flushed the pieces down the toilet.

All day long, she thought about the bill. She tried to concentrate in school, but Miss Marshall's voice sounded faint, like a distant wind. And although Tiffany frowned when she saw Martha, who had not one stripe on her at all, Martha didn't care. She ran all the way home by herself, thinking, thinking about the bill. How could she pay it?

She telephoned Winston again. This time he answered.

"Winston, it's me. I—"

"You hurt me. I just want you to know that."

"Oh, Winston, I *do* know. I'm sorry."

"I thought we were friends, but I guess I don't know everything, right?"

"We *are* friends."

"Sure. Well, I have to go. Got a test tomorrow."

Then he hung up so quickly that she didn't get a chance to tell him the bill had arrived, just as he'd wisely predicted.

Late that night Martha couldn't fall asleep. She tossed from the wall to the edge of her bed and back to the wall again, punching her pillow down as she worried in the darkness. Suddenly she sat straight up, remembering. Exercise Number Six. Of course.

Twelve

MARTHA could hear Winston practicing his clarinet as he did every morning, in his room above hers. She put her pillow over her head, but she could still hear his toots. Angry toots.

She didn't really see why he continued to be angry. Hadn't she apologized?

Winston was playing Brahms, reminding Martha of what she had planned to do that day. At her desk, on a big piece of heavy, white cardboard, she began to make a sign, choosing a different color felt pen for each letter.

It was so simple, she thought, as her pens squeaked. Sing your song, guitar player, the manual had told her. Almost too simple, really. Like when you're trying to reduce a fraction and you look at it and realize it's already reduced.

Martha finished her sign. It said:

THE FIFTY SONGS
OF MARIELLA EMERALD

She rolled it up into a long tube and secured it with a rubber band. Then she began to pack things into a big shopping bag. When she was done, she went out to the kitchen for breakfast.

"We have a surprise for you," said Martha's mother, smiling, "You tell her, Bernard."

Mr. Green put down his morning newspaper. "Well," he said. "Let's see if she can guess. What's bigger than a bread box?"

"Don't tease," said Mrs. Green, ruffling his hair.

Martha's father beamed. "Okay. On the spur of the moment, because the sun is shining and life is short and the rent is paid and there's love in our hearts—"

Mrs. Green giggled. "Bernard, come on!"

"We've decided that the three of us should spend this beautiful Saturday at—" Mr. Green paused dramatically and then he and Martha's mother cried out together, "Disneyland!"

"Who needs Tahiti when we've got Disneyland almost in our own backyard?" Martha's father exclaimed. "Pop was right. I've been walking around with a glum face too long, not remembering what's really important."

Martha was silent for several seconds. "I've got plans today," she said quietly.

"Plans?" said her father in a surprised voice. "What sort of plans?"

Martha shrugged. "Oh, just something . . . something planned ahead of time. Plans that can't be changed. I'm really sorry."

"Well, dear, if you've made a commitment to do something with a friend, we understand," said Martha's mother. "Would you like to invite the friend to come along?"

Martha looked down at her cereal bowl. "No," she said.

Spur of the moment. Why, oh why, couldn't it have been any other moment but now?

"Well, I guess there will be other times," said Mrs. Green in a cheerful voice edged with disappointment. Mr. Green went back to the worrisome news of the world with a solemn look.

When I return, things will be different, thought Martha.

On the number two bus, Martha figured it all out. Bee-Bob and Alula had earned twelve dollars for just one song. But then again, there were four people performing that day. Now she wouldn't have to share the money with anyone at all. Even if she earned only three dollars per song, that was three times fifty songs, one hundred and fifty dollars even, right there!

Martha leaned back in her seat, satisfied. When the bus stopped at Ocean Avenue, she hopped out, carrying her shopping bag, her guitar case, and her sign.

She found a spot on the beach, and from the shopping bag pulled out a blanket and the red nightgown she had worn on Halloween. She spread the blanket on the sand and put the nightgown on over her jeans and sweatshirt. She rolled up her sleeves and slipped seven bracelets belonging to her mother over her arms, and after removing her sneakers and socks, encircled the big toe of her right foot with her father's college ring. Then she took out her guitar, propped her sign against the open case, and began to play.

The beach was deserted. Martha remembered the music of Bee-Bob and Alula, how it filled the air and drew a crowd. She sat up very straight, like a queen.

One song sung, and only a chill December breeze whispered along the sand. Several sea gulls, but no people, sauntered by. Martha wriggled her cold toes. That was three dollars gone, she thought grimly.

Then, looking up, Martha noticed four distant figures walking briskly toward her. She began to play one of her favorite tunes.

"Silly young Bruce, with his big, fat goose, running away from the lonely moose," she sang with all her might, strumming loudly. Her bracelets clinked pleasantly to the beat.

The brisk walkers, four women, came into view. They held their elbows out from their sides, swinging their broad hips from side to side as they strode, brows furrowed in concentration.

This will make them pay attention and chuckle! thought Martha, as Bruce and the goose dodged a loose caboose. Sure enough, the walkers stopped. Martha finished the song with a pluckety-pluck flourish, returning Bruce and his goose home, safe and sound.

She waited for applause and laughter, but to her astonishment, there was none. Instead, one woman gave a windy sigh and another clucked her tongue.

A third woman approached Martha's blanket. She crouched down and laid a five dollar bill in the guitar case.

"Sweetie, are you all right?" she asked, sorrowfully studying Martha's nightgown and bare feet.

Martha pulled the nightgown over her toes in a dignified manner. "Of course."

"Tell us where you live, dear. We can take you home again. We'd like to help."

"I'm giving a performance," explained Martha, pointing to her sign. "Everything's fine."

The walkers looked at one another. The woman sighed loudly again.

"There's nothing more we can do, Charlene," said her friend.

Haven't they ever heard anybody jamming before? thought Martha, watching the three women march down the beach. Still, five dollars was five dollars, and now she was only one dollar behind. Martha straightened her sign, then picked up her guitar again. The show must go on.

"I'll take that," someone said.

A hand plucked the five dollars from the guitar case. Two arms snatched her guitar from behind. Turning, Martha caught her breath as she recognized her assailants.

The Halloween marauders.

"Well, well. Following you was worth a boring bus ride. Hand over the jewelry, too," said Web.

Martha was stunned. Had they been on the number two bus with her? She hadn't seen them. She stared at Web's T-shirt, at the evil-looking green spider perched on the web spreading across his chest, and felt dizzy.

"Come on, come on," said Cal, his two palms out, fingers wriggling.

Slowly, Martha slipped off her mother's seven bracelets and gave them to Cal, who stuffed them into his pockets.

"The ring, too," Cal said, gesturing toward Martha's big toe.

"Oh, no, I can't do that!" cried Martha. "That's my father's college ring!"

Cal looked interested. "Yeah?"

Martha began to talk very quickly. "The ring has a history in our family. My father's worn it for years and years, although not recently, since it's gotten a bit tight. And my mother wore it when they got engaged, but she hung it on a chain around her neck because it was much too big for her. It's a very special memento in our family."

"Hand it over."

Her hands trembling, Martha took the ring off her toe. She gave it to Cal, who put her family's very special memento on his own finger. Oh, how awful.

Cal made a fist and held his arm up. "Hey, look at this, Web! I'm in college!"

"Hah!" shouted Web, squeezing the guitar at its neck and swinging it over his hip. "You're in college like I'm a rock star!"

Web strummed the guitar hard, and it screeched as if crying for help. Horrified, Martha watched as he twisted his body up and down, strumming again and again, faster and harder until—twang!—a string broke. Web laughed and continued playing.

Martha jumped up. "Stop!" she shouted, running toward him.

Web grinned down at her. "Don't you like my music?"

"*That's* not music!"

"Oh, it isn't? Hmm, maybe you're right," said Web, nodding. "Maybe this cheap thing isn't even a guitar." He held it high over his head and swung the guitar in a wide arc, its broken string dangling forlornly. "It's a lassoooo!"

"Over here, Web," yelled Cal, his arms outstretched. "Give us a pass."

"It's a football!" shouted Web, throwing the guitar to Cal.

The instrument sailed through the air like a strange, purple bird, the string its tail, its sound hole a wide, scared mouth. Cal and Web pitched it back and forth, and as it flew by Martha, she heard its eerie cry. She began to run back and forth, too, jumping up high, trying with all her might to retrieve it.

"Here, kid, catch!" yelled Cal, throwing the guitar toward the sea.

Martha raced to the shore, but Web got there first. With a loud plop, the guitar landed on the wet sand. Web picked it up.

"Aw, shucks," he said. "All dirty. Needs a bath." Web crouched down and held the guitar toward an approaching wave.

"No, don't!" cried Martha. "You'll ruin it!"

Suddenly, a loud whistle pierced the air. Martha turned in its direction and saw Cal gesturing frantically. "Cops!" he yelled.

Striding resolutely toward them along the shore were the four walkers. They were flanked by two police officers, who broke into a run. Cal and Web bolted toward a bike path, bracelets spilling from Cal's pockets.

Shivering, Martha sat on the wet sand, cradling the guitar in her arms. The women approached and led her up to the dry beach. They wrapped the blanket around her shoulders and helped her with her socks and shoes, fussing and clucking like a flock of hens.

Thirteen

SHE was glad they had caught Web and Cal. Glad they got back the bracelets and her father's college ring, and the five dollar bill, which the woman had insisted Martha keep.

"You were lucky, Miss Emerald," an officer with kind eyes had said as she had made out the report in the police station.

"My name is Green," Martha had said in a shaky voice. "Martha Green."

She was even glad they'd phoned her parents. It was a gladness and a deep relief, as if old knots were being untied inside of her, even though their eyes were sad and frightened when they came to pick her up.

Martha huddled in the back seat of her parents' car on the way home from the police station, listening to the guitar case sliding back and forth, back and forth, inside the locked trunk. She wasn't really surprised when her parents said they had to mail it back.

Her father parked in spot 302 in the underground

garage and took the guitar case from the trunk. His face was solemn.

"What most concerns us," he said sternly as Martha stepped from the car, "is the lying, and the fact that you defied us."

"I know," said Martha. Her voice sounded small and whispery, as if it were disappearing deep inside of her.

"But, Martha," said her mother, "if you knew, then why did you do this? Why didn't you return this overpriced instrument, as you were asked to do? And panhandling to pay for it! Why, Martha?"

Mrs. Green's sad voice echoed hollowly in the cavernous parking lot. *Why? Why?*

"I guess I just liked it," Martha whispered.

Her father frowned. "We can't own everything we like, young lady."

Martha shrugged her shoulders and hung her head. How could she explain the guitar's specialness? She wanted to tell them how everything seemed to change for the better from the moment, the first exquisite moment she had played it and throughout the entire six-week free trial. Where were the words to make them understand?

That night Mrs. Green made Saturday spaghetti. It smelled inviting and familiar, but Martha had no appetite. She pushed her plate away and asked to be excused.

"Come here," said her father, and he pulled her up

onto his lap, as he used to do after dinner when she was little. Martha buried her head in his sweater and, fighting back tears, tried her best to explain about almost-empty photo albums when you're the youngest and better times long ago. There was a silence, and Martha knew that her parents were looking at each other, trying their hardest to understand.

"But, honey, you know we love you," said her mother. She stroked Martha's hair, while Martha's father hugged her harder into his sweater, his voice rumbling gently against Martha's forehead. He promised that she would have an instrument, a well-made one, and music lessons, someday soon when their budget could afford it.

After dinner Martha and her parents packed the guitar and the manual in the carton retrieved from the downstairs storage room. "Dear Sir or Madam," wrote Martha, "I am returning your guitar, for I cannot afford it. Thank you for the free trial. Enclosed is five dollars to pay for wear and tear. Sincerely, Martha Green." Then the box was taped up once again.

When the box was mailed and the guitar was gone forever, it seemed that more than the music had been sent away. All the magic it had brought had left, as well.

The evidence was everywhere. Martha's parents began to argue again. More than ever, Martha thought.

"I warned you your day was overly long! You need

to spend more time with her. She's much too unsupervised."

"*My* day! How could I think of cutting down my hours with you constantly griping about bills and debts? And can't fathers supervise their children?"

Martha could hear their harsh voices through the bedroom wall and feel their tension, like dry, gray smoke, filling up the rooms.

Day by day, an empty feeling grew inside her, a feeling that was quiet and dark and sad. She tried to hum snatches of tunes here and there, but that only made her feel worse. Oh, how she missed the guitar and everything that had come with it!

Grandpa Green missed it, too. "No music anymore? And no friend—what's his name?"

"Winston," she said. "I have new friends now."

"Ah, but old friends, old friends," said Grandpa sadly, looking out his window, "they're the best."

Martha noticed that he'd forgotten to shave, that dust was gathering on the bookshelves. Then, after their walk along the ocean, he started to hang up his raincoat in the refrigerator.

"Silly me," he said, turning toward the closet with an embarrassed grin.

And once, walking home from school with Tiffany and the others, she saw Winston get off a bus. He was deep in conversation with another boy from his school.

"There's your neighbor, Mariella," said Tiffany. "Where's his weirdo costume?"

"I never see him wear it anymore," Martha said. She wondered what interesting topic they were discussing, their heads close together, their hands moving in the air. Shakespeare? Spiders? The sociology of groups?

He may be weird, she should have said to Tiffany, but he's a wonderful weirdo. Come on, she should have said to all of them, I'll introduce you. He knows a lot about everything. He can keep a secret.

And tell me, she should have asked them, for now the question wouldn't go away, would you still be my friend if I were just plain Martha Green? Winston would.

One day, coming up in the elevator from the laundry room with a pile of towels in a basket, Martha met Winston coming in with a pile of books. The cover of one of the books showed a drawing of a heart with its arteries and veins.

"There's something I want to tell you," said Winston coolly.

The elevator stopped at Martha's floor. She stepped out, but held the door open with her laundry basket. She needed to talk to him, too.

"Just for your information, I'm having my operation after all. Very soon. The doctor said my heart is working too hard."

"Oh, Winston, I'm sorry!"

"No, I'll be fine. I'm tough as nails. This will make me even stronger, the doctor told me." Winston spoke firmly, but his eyes looked scared. He quickly bent down to push Martha's basket out of the way of the elevator door. "I'll be just fine."

Now she thought about Winston all the time, her worries for him crowding out thoughts of almost everything, even the guitar.

Ten days before the Holiday Fest, Tiffany called the popular girls together by the school-yard gate. "We've been waiting and waiting, Mariella," she said impatiently. "Haven't you chosen your song yet? What's taking you so long?"

Rosa spread her arms out wide, as if she wanted to hug the world. "Sing about keeping the earth green," she said.

"No, sing about peace," said Samantha.

"Love," suggested Courtney, a dreamy expression on her face. "Breaking up and making up again."

Tiffany frowned at all of them. "First we have to see how Mariella sounds. *Then* we'll decide." She turned to Martha, who stood silently at the edge of the group. "Why don't you go home and get your guitar?" she said. "Meet us at Jennifer's at four o'clock."

Martha walked home alone. She went up to her apartment, drank a glass of water, brushed her hair, then left for Jennifer's house, walking slowly. She had to tell the truth. There was nothing else she could do.

Jennifer's house, on the other side of the boulevard, was very, very large. Martha couldn't imagine what they did with all the rooms, since Jennifer's grown-up brothers and sisters lived somewhere else, and Mr. and Mrs. Okuda traveled to the Far East quite a bit.

A housekeeper in a uniform took Martha's sweater and gestured toward the living room. The meeting had already begun. Jennifer waved at Martha, patting the empty seat beside her.

Tiffany frowned, glancing at a big grandfather clock which said fifteen minutes past the hour. "As I was saying, it's very important that we all dress the same. If we don't, we'll look just like everyone else." Her eyes swept the room, stopping at Martha, who hadn't cared at all what she'd worn that week, then landing, finally, on Samantha Sampson.

"We agreed on polka dots, Samantha. Circles don't count," said Tiffany.

Samantha looked at her skirt, her mouth turning down at the corners.

But maybe it was all she had! thought Martha, stiffening. Maybe she had worried about it the whole night before, wondering if circles would make them angry at her. Maybe she had hoped they wouldn't notice. Maybe she had felt nervous and jumpy in class, thinking about circles instead of more important things.

"This is ridiculous."

"Excuse me?" Tiffany turned toward Martha. "Did you say something?"

Martha hadn't expected to say anything, but once she began, she couldn't stop. "I said it's ridiculous. Didn't you ever hear about the sociology of groups? It's group pressure and conformity, but most of all it's ridiculous."

Tiffany leaned over to the coffee table and surveyed the cookies on a silver tray, finally choosing a vanilla wafer. "Oh?" she said, chewing thoughtfully. "Let's vote on that. All those in favor of dressing any way they please, raise their hand."

Martha's hand shot up defiantly. Everyone else kept theirs clasped together, including Samantha, who was staring at her lap. Suddenly Jennifer, who was wearing the most beautiful dress Martha had ever seen, a glorious jumble of pink and yellow dots, raised her hand, too.

"Well." Tiffany looked at both girls angrily. "I can't believe it, J.O. And you, Mariella! Here we are, calling a special meeting just to help you, and you vote against us." Tiffany's eyes narrowed. "And where *is* that guitar, by the way?"

Martha took a long, quavering breath. "Gone," she said. "My parents mailed it back to where it came from. The six-week free trial was over, you see, and they said it wasn't worth the money to keep it."

Everyone was silent for several seconds.

"Gone?" whispered Jennifer.

Martha nodded. "Mailed back."

"See?" cried Tiffany triumphantly. "I was right! Didn't I keep telling you she was a show-off and an exaggerator? Fifty songs! What a joke! She never had a guitar and she wouldn't know how to play it if she did."

"Oh, yes, I would," declared Martha. "I took lessons from a book, but I *did* learn to play. And that's the truth."

Jennifer jumped up and ran from the room, the sound of her footsteps echoing against the lofty ceilings and splendid marble floors. When she returned she was carrying a brown guitar.

"My brother's," she said, holding out the guitar for Martha to play.

Martha took the guitar. The girls leaned forward intently as Martha stretched her fingers across its wide neck. "For my first song . . ." she said.

The grandfather clock bonged the half hour.

"Excuse me," Martha whispered, shaking her trembling hands. They felt so cold. "For my first song, I will play one of my favorites."

She stopped again. Which favorite? She could not think of a single, solitary favorite. She could not, in fact, think of a single, solitary song.

She placed her shaking fingers on the strings again. The room was quiet except for the tick, tick of the grandfather clock and a strange throbbing in her head.

" 'Old Macdonald,' " said Martha finally.

She looked up at the popular girls. They were all staring at her, except for Jennifer, who had her eyes closed tightly. Martha looked down at the brown guitar and realized that she could not play it. She stood up, leaning the guitar carefully against her chair.

"I'm sorry," she said, and ran out of the big room for home.

Fourteen

MARTHA woke up late the next morning. There were no strains of clarinet music from upstairs, and her parents had gone Saturday shopping for the day. She felt very alone. She decided to visit her grandfather.

On the front lawn of 356 Sandy Way, Martha saw a FOR SALE sign. Inside, boxes labeled BOOKS, DISHES, KNICKKNACKS, and MEMENTOS PRE-1933 were standing in the living room.

Speechless, Martha sat on a big picnic cooler in the middle of the room. That very morning, a young man had walked in and carted off the kitchen table and chairs for a good price, Grandpa Green told her. And Grandpa Green, Martha realized, would soon be carted off himself, to a senior citizen apartment-hotel. She wasn't really surprised.

"It's all my fault."

Grandpa Green, wearing a baseball hat backward on his head, was sitting on the floor, labeling another box, MEMENTOS 1933–1943. He looked up. "What? What nonsense is this?"

"If only I had told them. If only I had explained how you were getting better. Maybe then they would have let me keep the guitar. Grandpa, don't you remember how you started to remember, and then how you started to forget again?"

"I have my own ideas, but why don't you tell me yours?"

Then Martha told her grandfather the whole story, right from the very beginning of the six-week free trial; everything that had happened when she had the guitar, and everything that had happened when she no longer did. Down to the last nitty-gritty detail.

"So now they're carting you away, just like you said they would. Oh, Grandpa!"

Grandpa Green gave a little grunt as he pushed himself off the floor. He walked out the front door with Murray behind him. He immediately came back in and poked his head into the kitchen, then walked over to the picnic cooler where Martha sat. "So where is it?" he asked.

"Where's what?"

"The cart. Where's the cart?"

Martha sighed. "Grandpa, you know what I mean."

"There's no cart because nobody's carting me away!" cried Grandpa Green, shaking a finger at her. "Stop feeling so sorry for me. I made my *own* decision. I found my *own* apartment-hotel. When *I* was good and ready! And once I made up my mind, there was no stopping me." Then he began to chuckle, ignoring Martha's frown. "*Magic*! Martha, Martha. You've been watching too much television."

"I have not!" grumbled Martha, beginning to feel angry.

"Okay, okay. Understand, I'm a practical man. Magic isn't exactly my cup of tea."

Martha shrugged a shoulder at him.

"Move over," said Grandpa Green, sitting down beside her on the picnic cooler with a sigh. He took off his baseball cap and turned it over and over as if looking for a message written on it. "You know what I've been remembering lately, packing up all these boxes? I remember how you used to drive that talent lady, what's her name, absolutely crazy!"

"Mrs. Fifer?" Martha was aghast. "Grandpa! I did not!"

Grandpa Green nodded vigorously. "*Who* has a memory problem? Oh, what a time they had with you! 'This soup's *yucky*!' you hollered at the camera, and they had to shoot the whole thing again." Grandpa Green began to laugh until tears wet his cheeks. "We got such a kick out of that! What a lively little thing! You'd notice everything, good and bad." He paused to wipe his eyes with his handkerchief. "Well, the director and Mrs. What's-Her-Name didn't get such a kick out of it. But you *did* sell gallons of soup when you finally got it right. Or wrong, depending on how you look at it."

"I forgot about that."

"You said the soup had little green flecks floating in it, and you didn't like the taste," said Grandpa Green, still chuckling. "You finally agreed to sing because you liked to sing, but you kept your fingers crossed behind your back the whole time."

Martha laughed. "I did?" Suddenly she felt a happy rush of affection for the five-year-old, adorable Martha. An entirely different kind of adorable than she had thought, however.

Grandpa Green leaned over and gave her a kiss on the cheek. "So now you took up music again. And you started noticing things about yourself and the world again, some things good, some things not so good. What's so new about that? After all, you're still the same Martha you always were."

You're still the same Martha. She leaned against him. "Grandpa, I love you so much."

Grandpa Green nodded, giving her a teary wink. He pulled Martha against him. "Okay, you win," he said in a hoarse voice.

"Win?"

"I was lonely, and you made me less lonely. I danced, I sang, I remembered. Is that magic? One person making another person feel better, think better? Could be. But one day it occurred to me that telling stories to Murray the cat wasn't enough."

Grandpa Green jumped up and went into his bedroom, quickly returning. "Here," he said, handing her a shiny brochure.

Martha looked it over. "The Heritage Lodge. Quiet, efficient apartments, Early American decor. Billiard room. Large recreation rooms for dances and meetings. Nutritious meals served twice a day." She looked up, filled with relief for her grandfather.

"I can organize a club or two. Probably stir things up a little, once I get there," said Grandpa Green, grinning. He got up to let in Murray, who had been yowling at the door. "And they take pets, too."

How could she have forgotten such a funny story? Martha wondered, thinking about the TV commercial on the bus ride home. A story that told of such a brave part, such a *weird* part, actually, of her own self. She couldn't wait to tell Winston. She would phone him as soon as she got home. She'd tell him the story even if he was still mad at her.

Martha sat bolt upright in her seat, remembering that she had not heard Winston's music that morning and suddenly understanding what that meant.

As soon as she reached Mariella Manor, Martha hurried up to the Hoopers' apartment. She rang the doorbell and then knocked loudly on the door. No response! Martha ran down the stairs, burst into her own apartment, made a phone call, then burst out again. There was no time to wait for the elevator. She clattered down the stairs and ran out of the building, past Cynthia Corners and Gloria Gardens, five blocks south, four blocks west, all the way to the big, white, imposing hospital on the corner. She had never in her life run so far so fast. All she kept thinking about, over and over, was what her grandfather had said about one person making another person feel better. Science or magic, it really didn't matter.

"Winston Hooper, recently admitted." Martha leaned against the counter of the information booth, trying to catch her breath.

"Room 1289," said a guard. "Visiting hours are nearly over."

Breathing in the sharp hospital smell of rubbing alcohol and meal trays and flowers, Martha took the elevator to the twelfth floor. She stood in the doorway to room 1289. There in bed was Winston, pale and frightened looking, holding his Volpa headdress.

"You came!" he cried, sitting up.

Martha sat on the edge of his bed and took his hand. "Of course I came," she said. "How're you doing?"

"Pretty good. The operation's on Monday and I've spoken to all the doctors and nurses. Very competent bunch."

"Are you all alone here?"

"My mom went to get a cup of coffee. She's a mess, worrying all the time. She always treats me like a baby, but really, Marth, she's the one who's scared.

Well, I'm scared, too, but not half as much as she is."

"It's a big deal," said Martha. "You're her only child."

"Yeah. I know." He looked at Martha intently. "I'm glad you're here."

"You're my best friend," she said. "Of course I'd be here."

Winston's smile brought color to his cheeks. "Really?"

"I'm so sorry I said those things that day. You know more about friendship than anybody. And you didn't have to go to the Hollyhock Academy to learn about it, either."

"I really wanted to phone you before I came here, but I didn't want you to see how scared I was."

"Oh, Win, that's silly. You should have called. I'd be scared, too."

Winston pointed to the headdress on the bed. "I wonder if the doctors will let me wear this in the operation. Do you think that's weird of me, to want to wear it?"

"Absolutely not!" said Martha. "Volpa's your thing."

"I forgot to ask them."

"But even if they don't, remember what the Bard said. Your courage is right inside of you, ready for the occasion."

"Right. Thanks for reminding me. Hey, I thought you didn't like Shakespeare."

"He's growing on me." They grinned at each other.

"Are you all ready for the Holiday Fest?" Winston asked.

"All ready," said Martha softly. She just couldn't tell him the truth yet.

A nurse poked her head into the doorway to say that visiting hours were over.

"Just one more thing," said Winston, talking quickly. "I've always wanted to confess this to you, and now's the time. Here goes: I'm ashamed to admit I've never really seen your Souper Soup commercial, Marth. I only said I did because . . . well, I felt like I'd seen it because you talked about it so much."

"That's okay," said Martha. "The soup was yucky." And she told him the story Grandpa Green had told her, making Winston laugh.

"But listen," continued Winston, holding her hand tightly, "I don't think commercials are such a big deal, anyway. You'll be a bigger star when you're discovered. You already are a star, in my opinion, even if . . . even if you never . . ."

Martha smiled. "Thanks," she said.

"I'm glad you came." Winston leaned back against his pillow.

"Me, too. Everything will be okay. I'll see you very soon."

On the way home from the hospital, Martha was thinking about Winston and her grandfather and numinous occurrences. What if she met someone right then and there who said they were her fairy godperson? she asked herself. And what if that fairy godperson, with a wide sweep of a wand making music swell and silver sprinkles rain down, presented her with a guitar? Would she know how to play it?

Yes, Martha realized. Yes, she would, magic or not. And as Martha ran toward Mariella Manor, she was struck with an excellent idea, as if it were a gift out of the blue. She could already hear the music in her head.

Martha gasped as she entered the lobby of Mariella Manor. The room was resplendent with lights: red lights, green lights, blue and white lights, blinking on and off.

A big, jolly-faced woman in overalls stepped off a ladder. "Whew!" she said, wiping her brow with a tissue. "Some job, but I think we're all done. Well, what do you think?"

"It looks beautiful," said Martha, staring all around her.

The woman held out her hand. "Mariella Wittencorp," she said. "I inherited this property from my father, and now I've decided to manage it myself. After all, if it's named after me, I better make sure it looks good, right?" She laughed heartily.

Mariella! *The* Mariella.

"Martha Green," said Martha, shaking hands.

"Martha Green? I've been wanting to meet you!"

"Me?"

"Aren't you the one with all the suggestions?"

Martha nodded.

"Well, this is the result," said Mariella Wittencorp with a wide, bountiful sweep of her arm. "I think some holiday decorating around here is an excellent suggestion. Oh, and look at this." She pointed to a big bulletin board by the elevator. "For inter-tenant communication. Another good idea of yours."

Several days later, Martha pulled the Greens' mail from their mailbox: the usual assortment of bills and notices for her parents, as well as a medium-sized wrapped package for herself. It was from the Musical Enterprises company. She opened the package immediately.

To Martha's delight, her friend Ms. Manual smiled from the cover of the *Musical Enterprises' Winter Catalogue*. Inside its pages, the multitalented Ms. Manual tooted, fiddled, and pounded, with great energy and aplomb, a seemingly endless variety of brightly hued instruments. Piccolos, tubas, violas, snare drums, French horns, pianos, and flutes—Ms. Manual could play them all, proclaimed the catalogue, using "The Marvelous Modern Method based on The Five Human Senses!" Would *Martha Green* be interested in further free trials? Would any of *Martha Green*'s friends? There would be no obligation to buy.

Martha smiled to herself. Then she thumbtacked her notice to the bulletin board near the mailboxes.

ATTENTION MARIELLA MANOR TENANTS!

I am trying to save up money to help my parents buy me a guitar and to pay for music lessons. I am not a beginner. I love music and I enjoy singing immensely.

I live in apartment 302. I'm eleven and in sixth grade. (You may have seen me around.)

There are several things I can do:

(a) *Baby-sit.* I am responsible and good with children. Furthermore, my parents have promised they'll be home at a reasonable hour every evening except Wednesdays, and will be on call in case of emergencies.

(b) *Sing or read to shut-ins.* Also, I am a good conversationalist and listener. I play a bit of chess.

(c) *Clean up.* Do you have a closet or a desk or a room that needs tidying? I can do it.

(d) *Cook.* I have in my possession the recipes for seven tasty casseroles, but I am willing to try your recipes, too.

(e) *Entertain at parties and special events.* I occasionally play duets with my friend and fellow tenant, Winston Hooper, Apt. 402, who is an excellent clarinetist. He is recuperating nicely from a heart operation and will be available in the near future.

I shall pin up a recent photo of myself as soon as my parents finish their roll of film.

Please indicate your interest below.

Sincerely,
Martha Green

You may want to attend the Holiday Fest Concert at Cypress Tree Avenue Elementary School. I have borrowed a friend's brother's guitar and will be singing a song.